'Who the he[...] are?' Paula [...]

He chuckled. 'Y[...] Castle. I'm Franco's cousin. And I'm here to stop you in your tracks.'

For a moment he towered over her.

'I didn't mean to floor you,' he drawled, his eyes gleaming.

'Then I would be glad to know just what you did mean to do,' she told him coldly.

'Warn you off.'

Dear Reader

There's nothing more wonderful than celebrating the end of winter, with an exciting collection of books to choose from! Mills & Boon will transport you to all corners of the world, including two enchanting Euromance destinations—sun-drenched, exotic Madeira contrasting with scenic evergreen Wales. Let the spring sunshine brighten up your day by reading our romances which are bursting with love and laughter! So why not treat yourself to many hours of happy reading?

The Editor

Born in London, **Sophie Weston** is a traveller by nature who started writing when she was five. She wrote her first romance recovering from illness, thinking her travelling was over. She was wrong, but she enjoyed it so much that she has carried on. These days she lives in the heart of the city with two demanding cats and a cherry tree—and travels the world looking for settings for her stories.

Recent titles by the same author:

DECEPTIVE PASSION

TRIUMPH OF THE DAWN

BY

SOPHIE WESTON

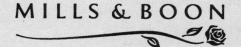

MILLS & BOON LIMITED
ETON HOUSE, 18-24 PARADISE ROAD
RICHMOND, SURREY TW9 1SR

*First published in Great Britain 1994
by Mills & Boon Limited*

© Sophie Weston 1994

*Australian copyright 1994
Philippine copyright 1994
This edition 1994*

ISBN 0 263 78421 5

*Set in Times Roman 10 on 11½ pt.
01-9403-52389 C*

Made and printed in Great Britain

CHAPTER ONE

PAULA heaved the door open with one shoulder and thrust her bulging briefcase through it. The heavy door, unimpressed, swung inexorably closed. It crunched the briefcase, dragging the overnight bag off her shoulder with its force.

'Damn,' said Paula excusably. She was clumsy with tiredness. Four trips across the Atlantic in ten days had left her head at thirty thousand feet and her stomach in New York, she thought wryly. But training told. She was, she reminded herself, a problem solver.

She put the briefcase and the little suitcase down neatly side by side. Then she rested her back against the brass-framed monstrosity which guarded the entry to her luxury block; and pushed with all her might.

'Allow me,' said an amused voice.

Paula looked up with a start. She had to look a long way up. The man in front of her was well over six feet: tall and dark as the devil, she thought, disconcerted by his sudden appearance. The strongly boned face was too cynical to be handsome, though. And, though he appeared to be amused just at the moment, he did not look as if he was kind in the general way.

The stranger put a long arm over her shoulder and flicked the heavy door open as if it were doll's-house furniture. Paula, who was not expecting the movement and was still leaning quite heavily against it, staggered. He caught hold of her elbow. She regained her balance, feeling a fool.

'Thank you.' Her voice was cool.

5

'My pleasure.' He still sounded amused, which wasn't, Paula thought sourly, very chivalrous. 'And these are yours?'

Without waiting for an answer he picked up the two cases—one-handed, Paula noted, trying to suppress irrational irritation at so much easy strength—and held the door open for her to pass in front of him. Shrugging slightly, she did so. But her thanks were not enthusiastic.

Paula looked at him covertly. He was walking into the block with every assurance but she did not recognise him as a resident. She would have remembered those powerful shoulders, she thought involuntarily. To say nothing of the great height and the shock of wavy hair so dark that it looked almost black. He was not the sort of neighbour you would meet in the lift, even if you went bleary-eyed to work as she had been doing recently, and not notice.

He was clearly thinking the same about her.

'Who are you visiting?' he asked, indicating the security door and the intercom beside it with its discreetly labelled bells.

For all it was a reasonably sized block there were only eight of them. The apartments were not only luxurious, they were big. It had been a real triumph to buy one in the new luxury block for which her firm was doing the conveyancing.

A measure of my success, Paula thought, as she had thought before. She wondered why, after all those years of effort and dedication, the success wasn't tasting so sweet these days.

'Number seven,' she said briefly.

After the penthouse, owned by some mysterious overseas millionaire whom nobody ever saw, it was the largest apartment in the block. She wondered if that was why his eyes widened a little. Her black suit was tailored and ultra-expensive but she had virtually lived in it for three days. He must be thinking she was too shabby to visit the luxury flat. As she would have been once.

'I live here,' she said, not without satisfaction. 'No point in ringing. Nobody's home.'

She fished out her security card to insert into the door. He was before her, though. She thought there was speculation in the dark face. But he opened the security door and ushered her inside and into the lift.

'Then we are neighbours,' he said pleasantly.

There was a faint, attractive accent to the clipped tones. Paula had so many international clients now that she began automatically to try to place it. Not French or any of the guttural languages. Spanish perhaps?

She sagged against the wall of the lift as the doors closed. She wasn't going to do *anything* when she got indoors: not look at the post, not listen to the messages on her answering machine, not so much as phone the office. And Trish's SOS could wait too. Paula didn't feel up to sorting out the latest of her sister's lame ducks until she had had a good sleep and a decent meal. She was going to shower and fall into bed.

The stranger said, 'We haven't met before, I think.'

With an effort, Paula pulled herself upright and re-focused her eyes.

'I travel a lot,' she said briefly.

'That would account for it,' he agreed.

He was looking at her oddly, she thought. Almost as if he was speculating about her; almost as if he found her attractive. The unchivalrous amusement had died out of his face as if it had never been there. It had been replaced by an odd intentness.

Paula stirred uneasily. It was not that she was unused to men finding her attractive. Her cool blonde beauty had distracted more than one of her legal colleagues in the past. But after Neil she had learned the hard way that she did not have the temperament to run the risks that went with personal relationships. She had become an expert in deflecting them.

Only, did she have the energy to raise the deflector shields now? she thought wryly. She looked at the tall figure under her lashes. Something warm seemed to trickle down her spine.

Startled, Paula came upright and prepared to freeze him. He had not yet pressed the buttons to get the lift moving.

'Third floor for me, please,' she said.

In the confined space he seemed even larger. He was looking thoughtfully down at her baggage. The labels had been overprinted and exit-stamped so many times that she had attached a leather-bound label to the handle with 'Ms P Castle, London' written in huge letters in dayglo scarlet.

Paula sighed. So now he knew her name. Still, if he was going to make a nuisance of himself, it didn't much matter, she reminded herself. Since he already knew where she lived, finding out her name would have been easy if he were determined. It was odd that she should have such a very clear impression that he was very determined indeed.

But all he said was, 'Flat seven. Of course.'

He pressed the button for the third floor. With her antennae alert, Paula noticed that he didn't press any other button. Damn.

Only then he looked up and for the first time she met his eyes.

She rapidly revised her impressions. Determined he might be, but he certainly didn't find her attractive. Whatever else this man might be contemplating, he was not going to press unwanted attentions on her. It was slightly unnerving, that cold, assessing stare.

She was being fanciful, she told herself at once. Tiredness and overwork had made her forget how real people behaved in normal social situations. He was simply a neighbour being cordial.

Except that those cold eyes didn't look cordial. They looked almost like those of some of the fellow lawyers she met in negotiations—good manners disguising latent hostility.

Now you really are getting paranoid, she told herself. To shake off the nasty feeling, she made an attempt at social conversation.

'Have you lived here long?'

His eyebrows went up. They were dark and strongly marked above steeply lidded eyes.

He said, 'I bought the penthouse some time ago. But this is the first time I have spent any time here.'

The penthouse. So here was the mysterious millionaire. Paula found she was not surprised. He had that air of unthinking command which she saw so often in her rich and powerful clients. She didn't like it. But she said civilly, 'Do you like the flat? It must have a wonderful view.'

A shrug of powerful shoulders dismissed the view.

'It is convenient,' he said indifferently.

For his wife to descend once a year to do her Christmas shopping in Harrods, no doubt, Paula thought waspishly.

Trying to disguise her instinctive prejudice, she said, 'Do you know London well?'

'I can find my way around.'

Which told her precisely nothing. He had the air of a man who would find his way around Mars if he happened to find himself there. Except that she didn't think he was the sort of man who often found himself anywhere he hadn't precisely planned to be.

Paula gave a little shiver. She must be more exhausted even than she realised. It was not like her to react so strongly to a man, especially one who had given her no cause. The arrogance and the coldness were as natural to him as breathing, she thought. He was not directing them especially at her.

She struggled with her party manners. 'Will you be staying long?'

The hard eyes swept over her. 'As long as it takes.'

Paula stared at him. It sounded like a threat.

I must see the quack, she thought. I'm light-headed. I've never got to the point where I thought perfect strangers were threatening me before.

The lift stopped and the doors swished open in expensive silence. He turned, taking up her cases again as if they were nothing, and gestured her out of the lift.

There was no help for it. Paula hesitated, then shrugged, obeying. If he wasn't attracted to her, he wasn't going to be difficult to get rid of. She could still have that shower and fall into bed at once.

She extracted her keys and unlocked carefully. The door wasn't double locked. That meant that Trish, not Isabel, her cleaning lady, must have been the last person to leave. Paula sighed. Her younger sister was lively and kind and the best of companions. She was also a walking dustbin. The last time she had used her spare key she had left the flat looking as if it had been hit by an earthquake. Isabel had been furious.

Paula turned to her companion, holding out her hand.

'Thank you for your help,' she said, wishing she sounded more sincere.

He shook his head at her hand.

'Then let me come in and complete it,' he said easily. 'I'm sure there are more doors you won't be able to open with these cases in your hands.'

If it hadn't been for those cold grey eyes, Paula would have stood her ground and said no. But it was so obvious that he wasn't attracted to her that she wasn't alarmed. Faintly annoyed at being kept from her shower and more than a little bewildered at her own acquiescence, she let him in.

The hall was full of mail. It was on the floor, on the telephone shelf and piled on the Elizabethan oak table underneath the great spreading arrangement of laurel and azalea that Isabel had left to greet her. Paula felt warmed by the gesture.

The tall, dark man said, 'Where would you like them?'

Paula turned back to him.

'Oh, if you'd just put them down in the sitting-room. Through there. I'll deal with them in there.'

She followed him into the room. It was long and sunny, eerily quiet in the afternoon sunlight. She walked over to the floor-to-ceiling French windows, unlocked them and slid one back. Even so, the noise of the traffic below drifted up very faintly.

She looked at the clock above the fireplace. Three-thirty, London time. Mid-morning in New York. Fourteen hours since she had eaten and she couldn't guess how many since she had slept properly.

Her uninvited guest put down her cases behind the large sofa and wandered out on to the balcony. He looked round at her tubs of spring bulbs.

'Very restful. Are you a gardener, Ms Castle?'

Paula gave a short laugh. 'I'm lucky if I'm here often enough to pick off the dead heads. My cleaning lady is the one with green fingers.'

He sat down on the pine bench against the far wall and tipped his head back to look at her. This year's growth on the clematis had taken it to the top of the trellis already, Paula noticed, looking at the plants that climbed the wall behind his head. The last time she'd been out here it had been barely up the back of the bench.

She sighed. So how long was it since she had been out here on her beloved balcony? Two weeks? Three?

'Quite charming,' he said, not taking his eyes off her.

To her surprise, Paula flushed. How could he make that clipped voice sound sensual? she thought, annoyed. But there was more than annoyance there as well. For some reason that she couldn't account for, the stranger made her feel vulnerable.

To dispel the illusion, she said crisply, 'I've only just got back after a tiring flight. If you'll forgive me...'

His mouth crooked into a smile. It didn't, she saw, reach his eyes.

'You want a cup of tea,' he supplied. 'You see how well I understand the English. Tea, the universal comforter. I have even developed the taste myself. I will join you.'

Paula stared at him, hardly believing her ears at this effrontery. Then, suddenly, it struck her as funny: she had come back blank with tiredness and was being manoeuvred into giving him tea like some Victorian aunt. Probably successfully.

She made one last, not very hopeful attempt to disengage.

'I've trespassed too much on your time already, I'm sure you must have hundreds of things you should be doing,' she said sweetly.

The grey eyes narrowed. She thought she saw the gleam of appreciation in them, though she couldn't be sure. Then the steep lids dropped.

He said smoothly, 'Thousands, rather. But I can still take the time to be neighbourly.'

Which very neatly lobbed the ball back on to her side of the net, thought Paula, admiring the tactic. If she

turned him out now she would look boorish and un-
grateful—and he would have walked off with all the
honours in the unspoken duel between them. She was
in no doubt now that it was a duel. Though she hadn't
the remotest idea *why*.

She toyed with the idea of saying she'd run out of tea.
But she was fairly sure that that would elicit a limpid
invitation to take tea in the penthouse. That was marginally less attractive than squaring up to him on her
home territory. She shrugged, conceding defeat.

'I'll put the kettle on.'

He didn't stay on the terrace while she was brewing
tea. He came back into the sitting-room and began to
prowl round it. She heard him take books off the shelves
and put them back. It gave her an odd feeling of being
dissected.

She went back with a tray and a renewed determination to have him out of the door as soon as decently
possible.

With perfect manners, he came forward and took the
tray from her. The courtesy was undermined by the faint
air of mockery with which he did so.

He said, 'You have some beautiful things. Family?'

Paula gave a small private smile. The only inheritance
she and Trish had received was an ugly brass Buddha
lamp-stand which they shuffled between them. Currently
it was in Trish's possession in her shared house in
Willesden. When she moved, as she undoubtedly would
all too soon, no doubt it would come back to Paula.
Trish was a percher, not a nest-builder like her sister.

'I just buy what I like when I see it,' Paula replied.

She found he was looking at her narrowly, the eyes
so cold and measuring that for a startled moment she
felt he had read her thoughts. For an instant their eyes
locked. It was unnerving.

He said softly, 'It must be very—pleasing—to be able to buy what you want when you see it.'

She had the feeling that for some obscure reason he was angry. She sipped her tea quickly and scalded her lip. Damn the man, why did he make her feel so nervous? She was behaving like a schoolgirl.

He had not touched his own tea. He was looking at her cases. He said, 'Business or pleasure?'

'Business,' Paula said. 'It always is with me, I'm afraid.' She thought about it for a moment and then added slowly, 'I can't remember the last time I took a holiday.'

'Conscientious? Or ambitious?' he asked. He didn't sound as if he would be impressed by either.

She laughed. 'A bit of both, I suppose. I set out just trying to pay the bills. But then I got interested. And I like to do a good job.' She shrugged. 'So I ended up living on planes. It wasn't what I set out to do.'

He was frowning slightly.

'What did you set out to do?'

Paula sipped her tea, debating with herself. It was obvious that he wasn't going to leave until he had found out whatever it was he wanted to know. Maybe, she thought on a flash of inspiration, he was one of those immensely rich men who wanted to vet the neighbours before he let his family move in, in case there were terrorists and gangsters in the block who might threaten them.

So she said equably, 'I wanted a decent qualification that would get me a job to keep my sister and me. Being a lawyer was just chance. It meant I could earn a salary of sorts during the day and do my degree in law during the evening.'

He sat upright suddenly. 'A *lawyer*.'

Paula was surprised. 'Yes. Sorry. Didn't I say?'

'I—had rather a different impression.'

He was angry again. Paula didn't know how she could tell. He was still courteous. But there were deep indentations from his nose to the corners of his mouth which made him look at her as if he was tempestuously angry inside. She didn't understand it and she didn't feel up to interrogating him. She passed a hand rapidly over her eyes, then shrugged.

'Sorry about that,' she said briskly and insincerely. 'I'm a solicitor. I specialise in international corporate law. Hence the planes. But quite safe and respectable.' She put down her cup and stood up. 'So you needn't worry about me slipping a bomb under your door.'

He didn't rise, though the dismissal was evident. He tipped his head back and looked up at her through narrowed eyes. Looking down at him, Paula met his eyes and flinched. It was like putting your hand inadvertently against a block of ice, she thought, startled.

'I'm not sure you haven't already,' he said. He was not laughing.

Thoroughly ruffled, Paula dropped her struggle with basic courtesy.

'I haven't the slightest idea what you mean,' she said coldly.

He gave a harsh bark of laughter and came to his feet. It was a lithe, powerful movement, somehow redolent of the suppressed anger she had detected. Which was, she thought, rapidly becoming unsuppressed. She squared her shoulders, ready for battle. He didn't intimidate her—she was used to battles in her work—but she had a fleeting, rueful memory of her ideal homecoming to restful solitude. She lifted her chin and waited.

'Not the *slightest* idea?' he echoed mockingly. 'Not the faintest suspicion? You know, I find that hard to believe; a bright lady like you.'

Either he was a madman, Paula thought, or there was something going on that she didn't know about yet. Of course it might turn out to be nothing to do with her. But all her training told her to say as little as possible and keep him talking. That way she might find out.

So she raised her eyebrows and said nothing. It seemed to infuriate him. He was not the sort of man, she saw, who lost his temper impetuously. He neither shouted nor swore. Though she could see very clearly that he wanted nothing less than her absolute humiliation, he made no move towards her. Whatever else she had to fear, she thought, physical violence wasn't on the agenda.

'Did you think Franco's family would stand by and watch?' he said in a lazy drawl. It was somehow more menacing than any of the polished verbal attacks Paula was used to facing.

She jumped. Menacing? Fear? *Her absolute humiliation*? What on earth was she thinking about? Tiredness must have stimulated her imagination to boiling point. The man had said nothing to make her think in this highly coloured way.

Get a grip on yourself, Paula, she thought. Melodrama like this went out with silent movies.

She blinked rapidly and said, 'Who is Franco?'

She encountered a look like a swordpoint. She began to revise her opinion on melodrama.

But the drawl was more pronounced. 'Playing games, Miss Castle?'

Her own temper began to rise. '*I'm* not. Are you?'

'Oh, no,' he said softly. He folded his arms over his chest and propped himself negligently against the mantelpiece. 'You'll find I take blackmail very seriously indeed.'

'*Blackmail*?'

The heavily marked brows rose. 'What else would you call it?' he asked politely.

Paula put a distracted hand to her head. The immaculate blonde hair was beginning to frond about her ears. Normally she would have pushed it back into place at once. Now she hardly noticed.

How could anyone possibly blackmail her, even if they wanted to? Her life was boringly blameless—except, if you stretched a point, for that nasty little episode with Neil, she supposed. And even that had hurt no one but herself.

She shook her head. 'But I have no secrets...' she said almost to herself.

Her unwelcome visitor moved sharply. She jumped, her eyes flying to that cold face. But he was impassive again.

He said softly, 'Now somehow I doubt that.'

His eyes were flat and grey like pack ice. Although he didn't move Paula's mouth went dry. She realised suddenly how alone they were in the quiet flat. And the tall man lounging against the fireplace gave every indication of being supremely unfriendly. Unfriendly and something else. There was an awareness that hummed between them like a telephone wire.

To Paula it was as alarming as it was unexpected. She had only felt that sort of physical pull once before; never in the middle of an exchange of blatant hostilities. Never instantly.

You shouldn't have let him in, said her inner voice. Get him out. Fast.

She summoned up all her poise and said in her best negotiator's manner, 'Look, can we get this clear? I've said I don't know what you're talking about and I don't. If you want to tell me, fine. If not, perhaps you'd go. I've had a long day and I'm tired.'

He tilted his head. The cold eyes swept her up and down in a clinical inspection that, to her private astonishment, brought the blood storming into her cheeks. She hadn't blushed when a man looked her over for ten years. But then men didn't usually look her over in that contemptuous way.

'How old are you, Miss Castle?' he said.

Paula stared.

'Forty-three? Forty-five?'

'Thirty-one,' she snapped.

His eyes gleamed. Too late she realised she had been deliberately provoked.

'And how old do you think Franco is?'

Paula sighed. 'If I knew who Franco was, I'd put in a bid,' she said sweetly.

'The way I hear it you already have.' His voice was dry.

He lounged away from the fireplace. She tensed. It had brought him uncomfortably close. To look him in the face she had to tilt her head back at a painful angle. Stubbornly she did so, refusing to give ground.

He said quietly, 'I advise you to be very careful, Miss Castle. I am not a foolish boy.'

'No!' she exclaimed in mock-surprise.

His brows rose. '*Very* careful. These tricks of yours may be very charming to some men. They don't amuse me.'

She said frankly, 'I'm not trying to charm you. I'm trying to get you to go. I've never met such a thick-skinned man in my life.'

For a moment she thought she caught a gleam of admiration in the icy eyes. If she did, it was immediately banished.

'Yes, I imagine I'm a tougher proposition than Franco,' he agreed.

Her temper went dangerously close to flash-point. Recognising it, she caught herself. Losing your temper lost arguments.

'Look, I don't know why you're so concerned about this Franco, whoever he is, but...'

'Don't you?' He looked amused. 'You're an intelligent woman, Miss Castle. As well as beautiful. It must be obvious why I'm concerned.'

That stopped her dead. She had been going to deny all knowledge of Franco but that casual, almost contemptuous compliment silenced her like a blow. He saw it. His eyes narrowed.

'You know, I would be interested to see what you would be like if you *did* try to charm me,' he mused. 'It could be enlightening.'

Briefly Paula closed her eyes. Her strategy didn't seem to be working. Instead of finding out what was happening, she seemed to be getting deeper and deeper into fantasy.

She opened her eyes and strove for a reasonable tone. 'What do you want?'

He surveyed her for an unnervingly silent minute. She could hear her pulses slamming with tension. Then he put out a hand in a lazy movement and touched the escaping tendrils that brushed her neck.

'I'm beginning to wonder,' he said slowly.

Something old and long-ignored in Paula turned over inside her and flexed itself. She tautened.

'What do you *want*?' Her voice cracked.

He ran a long forefinger down the side of her throat, uncurling the hair against her skin. She felt the movement through every nerve. Something that she assured herself was outrage flared in response. She took two instinctive steps back.

'Perhaps I am not as thick-skinned as you think,' he murmured.

She took hold of herself.

'Who are you?' she demanded crisply. 'What right have you to force your way in here and...?'

'Force?' The dramatic eyebrows flew up. He looked unforgivably amused. 'I was playing porter at the time, if you recall.'

Paula shook her head.

'Oh, no,' she said gently. 'You're not going to get away with that. You got yourself in here because you want something. Why don't you just tell me what it is—and then get out?'

He chuckled. 'Fighting words.'

Paula favoured him with a sweet smile. 'I *am* a fighter. I'm known for it.'

His amusement grew. 'I can believe it. You know, I confess you surprise me, Miss Castle.'

She shrugged. 'Should I be flattered?'

'There's not a lot that surprises me these days,' he said musingly. 'Yes, I think you should.'

'OK. I'm flattered. Now who are you and what do you want?'

'I am Eduardo——' he hesitated '—Mascherini,' he finished, watching her narrowly.

It meant nothing to Paula. But at least it solved the problem of the accent.

She said wearily, 'It would be a lie if I said I was pleased to meet you, Eduardo. So can we just move along a little? You were going to tell me what you wanted.'

He said, 'Franco Gratz is my cousin.'

That didn't mean anything to her either. She searched her memory because there was a faint echo of the name somewhere at the back of her mind. Gratz—a client? A friend of a friend? She dredged again. But nothing came. She shook her head.

'Clearly a close family,' she said drily. 'I take it he is the Franco you've been throwing at me ever since you conned me into giving you tea. What am I supposed to have done to him?'

Steep lids dropped over the cold eyes.

'I thought I might ask you that,' Eduardo Mascherini told her softly.

Paula turned away, shrugging again.

'Since I can't remember him, I'm not going to be able to help you.'

'Can't remember him?' he echoed. 'Come, Miss Castle. You can do better than that.'

She turned to face him.

'You must realise, Mr Mascherini, I see a lot of people. I never forget a face but I'm pretty average at names, I'm afraid. I could ask my secretary to see whether she has him in the diary...'

Something in the cold face brought her to a halt. But all he said was, 'I can sympathise. I tend to need a memory jogger myself.'

He strolled towards her. Paula stood her ground but it was matter of pride that she did so. Suddenly she was quaking again. For no *reason*, she thought, despising herself.

He said conversationally, 'What do you think it would take to bring back Franco to your memory, Miss Castle? A photograph? I regret I haven't seen them yet, but I'm told they're quite something.'

She gaped at him. The voice, smooth and cold as toffee ice-cream, went on remorselessly.

'The diamonds? I, as you must know, haven't got them but presumably you have them tucked away somewhere safe in this tasteful apartment of yours? Shall we go and find them—and see if you can remember the man who gave them to you?'

He put his hands on her shoulders. Paula was so dazed that she didn't even protest.

'*Gave* . . .?'

He shook her slightly. A hairpin came adrift from its moorings and slipped down the back of her blouse. Paula barely noticed.

'Don't play the innocent with me, Miss Castle,' the dark stranger said harshly. 'It doesn't suit you. And I know the truth.'

'Well, I'm glad one of us does,' Paula said involuntarily.

The hands tightened painfully on her slim shoulders. She winced. Eduardo Mascherini seemed not to notice. His eyes were boring into hers.

'You never forget a face? I am nothing like my cousin, of course. What about a kiss, Miss Castle? Can you remember them? If you concentrate?'

Paula glared at him. 'Of course. I——'

'Good,' he said with a smile like a whiplash. 'Concentrate, then.'

He kissed her. Her hair finally fell down.

CHAPTER TWO

DAZED, Paula clung on to the only source of support in a tilting world. It chanced to be his shoulders but she was beyond caring.

She should have been affronted; angry. Maybe even a little alarmed. Instead, her whole body gave a small sigh, as if it had come home—and melted. *Definitely* light-headed, she thought.

She sensed his surprise. The arms around her tightened painfully. The searching kiss deepened. She felt his fingers in her hair. Then he was cupping her head as it fell back under the intensity of his kiss. Her throat arched and she drew a little ragged breath. Her eyes closed.

She felt weak, helpless, adrift in the middle of a powerful river with no hope of resistance or rescue. At the same time she was aware of a strong sense of recklessness as if she had chosen to throw herself in.

I must have gone crazy, she thought. All the overwork. They said it would catch up with me in the end.

Scarcely aware of what she was doing, she unhooked her clutch on the powerful shoulders and cupped his head between her hands. She was separately aware of the tentative butterfly nature of the touch, the roughness of his skin under her sensitive fingers; and a surge of energy like an electric shock in the bloodstream. Paula gasped.

That was when he went out of control. Paula was certain that up to that point he had known quite well what he was doing. She was not so dazed that she didn't recognise the strong element of calculation in that powerful embrace. She might have startled him with her

response but she had not rocked him off his intended
course.

But he was rocked off it now. His hands moved swiftly,
sweeping the length of her spine. She was moulded
against him like a shadow: dimensionless, voiceless,
without volition. There was no mistaking the explicit
hunger in his kiss nor the intent in the hard hands.
Vaguely Paula began to realise that she was out of her
depth, though she had neither the strength nor the will
to struggle.

Without releasing her mouth, he lifted her easily, one
hand like a bar behind her shoulders, one under her
knees. Paula clutched at him again, alarmed. He lifted
his head. She thought he gave a soft chuckle but she
couldn't be sure. Her eyes flew open.

He deposited her on the sofa and was beside her in
one fluid movement. He reclaimed her mouth. Paula felt
his hands at her waist, dealing rapidly and expertly with
fastenings. As her clothes loosened and began to fall
away, a measure of sanity returned. She put her hands
flat against his shoulders and pushed with all her re-
maining strength. Even to her, it felt as if it had about
as much force as a kitten's bid for freedom out of a
restraining human hand. It had no noticeable effect in
ridding her of that towering body. But it did make him
raise his head.

'Don't,' said Paula. It was not much more than a
whisper.

He looked down at her quizzically. She gathered her
forces.

'I mean it. Let me up,' she said, answering the look.
It was a croak.

One dark eyebrow rose. The grey eyes weren't cold
any more, though she didn't like the look in them any

better. They fixed on her mouth and he gave a soundless laugh. For the first time, Paula began to feel afraid.

Struggling against the unhelpful cushions, she managed to drag herself into a sitting position, one arm locked against his chest. Her hair was tangled and flopping about her face but she wasn't going to push it away. She needed all her concentration for her opponent. It didn't help that he was all too obviously aware of her disarray and amused by it.

One of the cushions fell squashily to the floor. Startled, Paula tilted. His eyes gleamed. Before she knew what he was about, he had tipped her back again and was touching a line of tantalising kisses up her exposed throat. Another cushion tumbled.

Paula thought hard thoughts about interior decorators and tore her mouth away.

'Let me go,' she yelled.

She hadn't shouted like that since she was a child. It startled her.

It startled him too. At least enough that he loosened his hold. Paula flung herself sideways in an inelegant scramble under his arm and found herself on her knees among the cushions on the carpet. She was breathing hard and her hair was everywhere.

He leaned back on his elbow and looked at her. Their eyes were almost at a level. He was looking interested. Paula ran a shaking hand through her hair, trying to smooth it.

'Who the *hell*,' she said between her teeth, 'do you think you are?'

He chuckled. 'Your briefing isn't very good, Ms Castle. I'm Franco's cousin. And I'm here to stop you in your tracks.'

Paula shook her head helplessly. He watched her in steely amusement. She began to have the nasty feeling of being adrift out of her depth again.

'Get out,' she said swiftly.

She hadn't very much hope that he would comply. Nothing she had said so far had had any noticeable effect on him. But to her surprise he lounged to his feet.

For a moment he towered over her, his expression unreadable. Their eyes locked. Paula felt her head begin to swim and took hold of the edge of the sofa. She realised suddenly how undignified she must look, crouching on the floor at his feet like this. She drew a deep breath—and found he was holding out a hand.

'I didn't mean to floor you,' he drawled, his eyes gleaming.

She ignored the hand. With what dignity she could muster, she stood up.

'Then I would be glad to know just what you did mean to do,' she told him coldly.

He smiled. Not nicely.

'Warn you off,' he said in a cool voice.

Paula glared at him. 'Consider me warned. Totally. Repelled to the nth degree. I'll never lay a hand on you again except in anger. I'll even let you have it in writing.'

There was a sharp little silence. Then he gave a shout of laughter and his smile changed.

'You know, you may be a scheming bitch, Miss Castle but you are not without your entertainment value,' he told her. 'I'm surprised, I confess.'

'Great,' Paula said affably. 'So flattering. I'm overwhelmed.'

His look was thoughtful. 'No, I wouldn't say that. A little—taken by surprise, shall we say? Rather like myself.'

Paula had no doubt at all what he was talking about. Her crazy, total response had startled her quite as much as him. She sniffed, trying to ignore the faint colour she could feel stinging her cheeks.

'Jet-lag,' she said firmly. 'And shock. I wasn't expecting to be jumped on.'

His lids drooped lazily. She saw he was laughing.

'Then you should have been,' he murmured.

Before she realised what else he was going to do, he had brushed one fingertip across her lower lip. There was something so proprietorial, so utterly negligent in the caress that Paula forgot her embarrassment in white-hot rage.

'Now I've met the neighbours,' she told him with poisonous sweetness, 'I will.'

He laughed. 'Splendid.' And hauled her into his arms again.

This time she was not so unprepared. She kicked him viciously on the calf and half twisted away. Reaching out, she pulled the portable telephone to her.

'Get out or I'll call the police,' she told him breathlessly.

He looked down at her, assessing.

'I mean it.'

'I can see you do.'

But still he didn't let her go. Paula decided on a high-risk tactic.

'And I'll tell Franco how you've pushed me around.'

His face seemed to freeze. Then slowly and deliberately he let her go as if she made his hands dirty. He stepped away from her.

'Do that,' he said.

He went to the door. Paula sagged slightly against the wall, the hand holding the phone falling loosely to her side. He opened the door and turned to look back at her.

'And *I'll* tell him,' he said in a voice like ice, 'that if I'd wanted to I could have had you here on the carpet. And you couldn't even remember his name.'

The disgust was palpable. He looked at her for a long moment. Paula felt herself whiten. Then the door closed very gently. He was gone.

Paula sank on to the carpet, clutching the telephone against her as, in the past, she had clutched her stuffed panda. Now he was gone, she felt shaky, close to tears and strangely hurt, although she had no idea what his accusations had been about. The palms of her hands were icy. She was trembling.

Her long-desired rest began to recede. For one thing, she needed to know who he was and why he had thought he had the right to treat her like that. For another she was much too wrought up to sleep. And she had needed that sleep.

'Damn him,' said Paula out loud.

It made her feel better. She said it again, fiercely, then uncoiled herself and stood up stiffly. She could call the office, even if she was not up to sorting out Trish's problems just yet. They were usually painful and complex and Trish thought Paula could solve them with a wave of a wand.

She settled in the corner of the sofa, wincing as she picked up the tumbled cushions. She hugged her knees, extended the radio aerial and punched in the office number.

Her secretary was unsurprised at the call.

'Hochfelder rang,' she told Paula with satisfaction. 'He's having the final contract couriered over tomorrow for Sir Basil's signature. He didn't sound pleased.'

Andrew Hochfelder was the negotiating partner on the other side in New York. Paula wasn't surprised that he was displeased. The compromise solution that she had proposed and sold to both parties would inevitably cut his fees. She gave a little laugh.

'That's post-meeting pique. He'll have convinced himself it was all his own idea in a week,' she said indifferently. 'Anything else?'

'Geoffrey has been in touch with Sid about the Australian idea,' Sarah said cautiously, mindful of the open line.

Geoffrey was their code name for the finance director of a major French corporation which was currently considering making a bid for a troubled Australian company.

'Sid said he'd talk to you first thing. Shall I send the papers round?'

'You'd better,' said Paula without enthusiasm. 'That it?'

She could hear Sarah consulting her computer message facility.

'Yes, everything else is in hand. Except your sister called again.'

'I know. She left messages in New York too. She didn't say what it was about, I suppose?'

Sarah hesitated. Then she said carefully, 'I'm not sure—I may be over-reacting—but I thought she sounded pretty upset.'

Paula's heart sank. Trish was altogether too softhearted, she thought. What had her sister got herself into now?

'All right, Sarah. I'll ring her now,' she said, bowing to the inevitable.

Trish was at work. When Paula was put through to her she sounded subdued.

'What's wrong, pet?' Paula asked.

Trish's voice thickened perceptibly. 'I can't talk about it now. I'm—a bit busy. Could I come over? This evening? I know you're probably jet-lagged but I must talk to you.'

She sounded composed enough but to Paula, who knew her better than she knew anyone, the suppression of a powerful emotion was evident.

'Of course,' she said swiftly. 'When? Do you want to come round after work?'

'I can get away as soon as I've finished this,' said Trish, normally the most conscientious, if not the most efficient, of employees. 'I'll come straight away after that.'

Paula's heart sank. This sounded like bad trouble. But she said calmly, 'Fine. See you then.'

She rang off and clipped down the aerial with a vicious movement. If someone had hurt Trish... She punched a cushion. Trish was too gentle for her own good, that was the trouble. She got too involved. And then she got hurt. Paula had learned not to get involved at an early age. But she had never managed to persuade Trish to follow her well defended example.

She sighed and stood up, stretching. Well, at least Trish had her. At her age, Paula had had no one.

She took the case into the bedroom and distributed its contents rapidly between the laundry basket and the bathroom shelf. She took off her suit, which would need to go to the cleaners. Isabel would deal with that tomorrow.

She looked at her slim gold watch. She had time for a shower before Trish arrived. She stripped off the rest of her clothes and stepped under the shower with a sigh of relief. Normally she would have had to loosen her hair, but of course the unwelcome stranger had done it for her. She rubbed shampoo into her hair, shivering under the stream of warm water. She wished she did not remember how she had felt with his hands in her hair. He had made her feel things she didn't think she had ever felt before.

'Jet-lag,' she said out loud. And got a mouthful of shampoo for her pains.

That, she thought, reluctantly amused, will stop me talking to myself in the shower. She rinsed her hair and soaped her body briskly. She had to put the man out of her mind.

He was crazy. Or no, he wasn't crazy—she'd never heard of a madman as cool as he was—but he thought she was someone else. Or he had heard half a story and leaped to some off-beam conclusions. It was a case of mistaken identity and she wouldn't hear from him again.

Which, Paula assured herself, rinsing her hair vigorously, was exactly what she wanted.

She was busy congratulating herself that she wouldn't have to see the disturbing stranger again when the doorbell rang.

At first she didn't believe it. Trish *couldn't* have got here this quickly. At least not unless her impecunious sister had taken a cab, which she never did. The bell rang again, insistently.

Quite suddenly Paula was really alarmed. It would have to be life and death to get Trish to spend money on taxi fares—or walk out of her office in the middle of the afternoon. She grabbed a towelling robe from the back of the bathroom door and a towel for her hair; and ran. She was still winding her sodden blonde locks in the towel when she opened the door.

It was not Trish. It was the stranger. Mascherini or whatever he said his name was.

All Paula's anxiety bubbled over in an explosion of anger.

'What the hell do you want this time?' she shouted at him.

He looked taken aback.

She knotted the towel angrily. 'You're not coming in, so don't think you are. You've had enough fun at my expense for one day,' she told him between her teeth. 'How *dare* you come back here, harassing me in my own home?'

His eyes narrowed. Paula refused to be intimidated. She stood her ground, though she took a good strong hold on the edge of the door at the same time.

Eduardo Mascherini said astonishingly, 'I owe you an apology.'

Paula stared at him. A faint flush appeared along the high cheekbones. She saw it with satisfaction.

'You're damned right you owe me an apology,' she agreed.

His face stiffened. He looked at her with acute distaste.

'I was under a misapprehension.' His voice became clipped, the accent pronounced. 'I saw your luggage label. You call yourself Miss P Castle. Since it was a Miss Patricia Castle whom I—er—needed to speak to and she also lives here, I am afraid I assumed you were she.'

Paula's heart sank to the bottom of her bare toes with a bang. Was *this* the man who had Trish sounding as if the world was about to come to an end?

Oh, Trish, this one's out of your league, she thought. What on earth have you done?

None of this, however, appeared in her manner. Eduardo Mascherini might, perhaps, have noticed that the slender fingers gripping the edge of the door whitened. But his eyes were too firmly fixed on her face and the pale skin revealed by the old and sloppy robe.

Paula kept her face neutral and promptly re-tied the sash of the robe so tightly that it hurt.

'And how did you work out that you had made a mistake?' she asked sweetly.

'It doesn't matter.' He had observed her wrenching at the sash and his lips twitched in spite of the stiffness of his expression. 'I only wished to make my apologies to yourself——' he gave her a stiff little bow '—and to ask that Miss Patricia Castle telephone me on this number.' And he produced a little piece of white card, blank except for a number scrawled in arrogant black script.

Paula took it slowly. She turned it over. There was nothing on the other side. Nothing to say who he was, where he lived or anything about him.

She said contemptuously, 'I'll give her your message. But if she asks my advice, I'll tell her to forget it.'

His eyes became steely.

'Then you would be very unwise.'

Paula shrugged. The robe slipped down one shoulder. The steely eyes followed it. For some reason it seemed to increase his anger. That pleased Paula, so she did not haul the robe back into place. Instead she met his eyes defiantly.

'And she would be equally unwise if she did as you suggested.'

Paula raised her eyebrows. 'Threats, Signor Mascherini? Are you going to blackmail my sister now, instead of me?'

'So she's your sister,' he mused. 'I wonder how much you have in common?'

For some reason that sounded as if it was intended to be an insult. Paula glared at him.

'You won't find she's any more susceptible to blackmail than I am.'

Mascherini gave a harsh laugh.

'You mistake, Miss Castle. It is I who am being black-mailed. By your sister.'

'*What*?'

Paula began to revise her opinion of his sanity, after all.

'You're out of your mind,' she said with conviction. 'Get out of my apartment.'

'I am not in your apartment—on this occasion,' he pointed out frostily. 'And I will go with pleasure. But I am not out of my mind, I assure you, Miss Castle. In fact I advise you to ask your sister about her relationship with my cousin Franco.'

Paula shrugged again. Trish was as pretty as she was loving. It was an occasionally lethal combination which Trish was not hard enough to deal with properly.

'If he's fallen for my sister he's neither the first nor the last. He'll get over it,' she said indifferently. 'I shall certainly not interfere. I'm not her keeper.'

His narrow-eyed look was hostile.

'She makes a habit of announcing herself to be pregnant by rich, inexperienced young men?' he asked politely. 'And it doesn't worry you?'

'Pregnant?' Paula echoed, shaken.

He relented a little. 'So you didn't know?'

'I don't believe it,' she said, more to herself than to him.

Was this why Trish sounded so choked and desperate? But how could she have formed a relationship so important that she made love with this Franco without telling Paula? Trish wasn't secretive and when she was in love it showed.

He nodded. 'No more do I. I think it is a clever device to extract money from a boy who doesn't know much about the world or people like your sister. But I am not a boy, Miss Castle. And neither of you will extract money from me.'

Paula hardly heard this.

'How long have they known each other?'

Eduardo Mascherini's mouth compressed to a thin line and the indentations on his cheeks became pronounced. He looked like a tyrant about to give sentence, Paula thought, noticing it and startled.

'A good point, Miss Castle. I asked as much myself. Franco tells me that they met at a party here. He does not remember who was giving it, which I find interesting. Your sister spent the night with him afterwards. It was the only occasion on which they slept together. I have pointed out to him the statistical unlikelihood of pregnancy resulting. But your sister has quite convinced him.'

Paula stared at him.

'A one-night stand—my *sister*?'

'So it appears.'

'Nonsense,' she said with absolute conviction. Under the outrageous accusation she had become oddly calm. 'I'm sure you believe you're telling the truth, Signor Mascherini. But there has to be some mistake. Maybe someone was using her name or something. It wouldn't have been Trish. I know her.'

He frowned quickly. Paula made to shut the door.

'I'll give her your message. Maybe she'll call you. But you'll find it's all a mistake,' she said firmly.

She shut the door on his protest, but half expected him to refuse to go. She stood in the small hallway, braced for furious ringing on the doorbell. But nothing happened. Perhaps he was sufficiently ashamed of himself not to make any further disturbance, she thought. It didn't sound convincing.

She climbed into fresh underwear, silky trousers and a loose top. Then she towel-dried her hair and ran a comb through it. Although it was so soft, it was thick and took a long time to dry. She left it loose on her shoulders and was debating whether to use her tiny blow-drier on it or not when the doorbell rang again.

This time it was Trish. One look at her and Paula held her arms open. Trish tumbled into her embrace and the floods broke loose.

'There,' said Paula, helplessly, patting the shaking shoulders. 'There.'

Eventually the storm subsided. Trish straightened, blew her nose and mopped the streaks of tears from her cheeks.

'Sorry,' she offered.

'What else are older sisters for?' Paula said, leading the way over to the sofa. She looked at Trish searchingly. 'Do you want to talk?'

'Or just howl?' Trish said with a watery attempt at humour. 'It's OK. I'm better now. I haven't really cried before and I suppose it all built up.'

Paula sat down. She slipped off her shoes and pulled her feet up under her. After a moment Trish slipped down on to the rug, her arm along the seat of the sofa. Her head drooped.

'What's the matter?' Paula prompted quietly. 'Can I help?'

Trish looked up at that. Her eyes were still swimming but she made a brave attempt at a smile.

'I doubt it. I've been stupid. Worse than stupid.'

She sounded much more than her twenty-one years, thought Paula, startled. She had a strong impulse to gather her sister up in her arms again. She resisted it. They had made a pact about Trish's independence when their father died; and Paula kept her promises. So in-

stead she tucked her hands inside the soft folds of her
sleeves and waited.

Eventually Trish gave a long sigh.

'You're not going to believe how stupid I've been. All
the things I said I wouldn't do,' she said bitterly. 'A man,
of course.'

She looked up quickly, faint colour in her cheeks. She
met Paula's eyes.

'You warned me,' she said. 'I know. I never thought
it would happen to me. I thought it was your fault that
you and Neil—I thought you were too prickly, too demanding, too suspicious. I thought you didn't give him
a chance. I'm sorry, Paula.'

Paula dismissed it with a gesture.

'You and I are completely different,' she said carefully.

There was no way Trish could have told that inside a
slow anger was beginning to burn against the unknown
man who had put those extra twenty years on Trish's
pretty shoulders.

'You couldn't be expected to run your life by my rules.
What works for me won't necessarily do for you. And
vice versa.'

Trish gave another of those heartbreaking attempts at
a smile.

'Thanks, Paula. But I know I should have listened to
you.'

She seemed unable to go on. There was a pause.

'What's his name?' Paula asked softly at last. 'Where
did you meet him?'

'Here,' Trish said. 'In the flat, I mean. Mrs Diaz asked
me to a party when she saw me in the lift. I was getting
some stuff for Isabel and I'd called round with it . . . Oh,
it doesn't matter, I suppose,' she said, running her hands
through her hair. 'He was at the party. I think I'd sort

of been asked for him, because he was the only one near my age. All the rest were even older than you.'

'Gosh,' murmured Paula.

But Trish was too deep in her story to register the irony. And as she went on Paula could hardly blame her.

'He didn't know anyone. And he didn't speak English very well. He'd only just arrived. He seemed—lost.'

Paula shuddered. She could picture the scene only too clearly. The young, uncertain stranger and Trish, little mother of all the world, bundling in to take care of him. He would not have been able to believe his luck. He would have seen the perfect figure, the long eyelashes and the sapphire eyes and he would not have noticed the real sweetness. Or the innocence. He would have grabbed whatever he could get, Paula thought. The anger had risen to a steady flame.

'So you took him under your wing,' she said. 'Then what?'

Trish hung her head.

'Tell me,' Paula said gently.

'We saw a lot of each other. We wanted to be together. You were away.'

'You brought him here,' Paula said in a carefully neutral voice. Well, that explained why Mascherini had assumed it was she who was conducting the affair with his cousin. 'He stayed nights?'

Trish swallowed. 'Yes.' She blew her nose again. 'In a way. He'd go home before Isabel came.'

'I see.' Paula digested this.

Neil, too, had been in the habit of going home in the small hours. It was because they had to be discreet, he'd said. It was only later that Paula had realised that the discretion was necessitated because he had a fiancée and the fiancée had a rich and influential family.

And now some playboy had sold the same line to warm and trusting Trish. The flame became white-hot.

Eyes like drowned forget-me-nots searched her face.

'Are you angry with me?' Trish asked.

Paula curbed herself. 'I haven't made such a success of my own life that I have any right to criticise you for yours,' she said honestly. 'As you very well know. Anyway, I suspect you're going to have to pay quite enough for it, without me setting myself up as judge and jury.' Her voice gentled. 'That's not all, is it, Trish?'

The tears brimmed over again.

'No,' said Trish in a whisper, hugging herself.

'Want to tell me?'

Though Paula was all too horribly sure she knew already.

'I'm going to have a baby,' said Trish, and began to weep in earnest.

She sat huddled against the side of the sofa, her face buried in her hands, her slender shoulders heaving. An anxious Paula found she could do nothing. Neither a hug nor words of comfort seemed to get through to the grief-stricken girl.

In the end, despairing, she made a mug of tea and pushed it into her sister's hands. The story, when Trish could get it out, was simple and very nasty.

At first it had not occurred to her that she might be pregnant. When it had, she had taken a test that proved positive. She had tried to tell Franco at once. She'd thought he would want to know... She had been intercepted by a woman. She didn't know who she was, except she was very glamorous and very angry and refused to let her see Franco.

So Trish had left a note, telling him everything. For days she'd waited for Franco to call. When he hadn't, she'd sent him another note—to his office. This time there had been a reply—from his secretary. He had gone out of town and wouldn't be able to see her. Since then she had heard nothing.

'You will,' said Paula, thinking of Eduardo Mascherini who thought Trish was a blackmailer and saw no reason to keep his predatory hands off blackmailers. That she, Paula, had briefly responded to him somehow made it worse. 'His cousin was here.'

Trish's sudden look of hope was more than she could bear.

'*Not* with friendly intent,' she said harshly.

Trish whitened. She looked as if she had been beaten.

I'll kill them both, Paula vowed.

CHAPTER THREE

PAULA didn't tell Trish the whole of her dealings with
Eduardo Mascherini, in the end. For one thing, she
didn't think Trish was ready for it. For another, she
wasn't quite sure how she was going to explain her own
reaction to the man.

As it was, she told her sister enough to startle Trish
out of her self-absorption.

'You let him just barge in here?' Trish said unbeliev-
ingly. 'Not knowing him? *You*?'

'He's a difficult man to say no to,' Paula said grimly.

Trish looked appalled. 'But he could have been a
burglar. Or anything. You were taking a terrible risk to
trust him.'

'I did not—and do not—trust him,' Paula said with
precision.

'But——'

'I told you, he didn't wait for my permission,' Paula
snapped. She bit her lip, then went on excusingly, 'I was
tired and he's very overbearing. Next time,' she added
vengefully, 'I'll have him thrown out before he puts a
foot over the threshold.'

Trish gave a watery giggle.

'You can't have him thrown out until he's got in,' she
pointed out reasonably.

Paula gave a reluctant smile. 'I can try.'

Trish squeezed her arm. 'Maybe you won't have to. I
shouldn't think he'll come back. Not now he knows I
don't live here.'

Paula frowned.

41

Trish said in her soft voice, 'This is my problem, Paula. I've got to sort it out myself. Don't get stuck in the middle. Especially if this Eduardo is such an ugly character.'

Paula thought of the broad shoulders and those lines of cynicism scored down the handsome face.

'Oh, he's that all right,' she said with conviction.

Tessa shook her head, bewildered.

'I don't understand. Franco seemed so gentle. He never talked about tough relations. He never talked about himself much at all...' Her voice grated and she stopped. Swallowing, she went on, 'I must try to see him again. He—he has a right after all...'

Paula couldn't bear the hurt in Trish's blue eyes. She said fiercely, 'He has no rights whatsoever. Don't you go near him. I'll deal with this.'

Trish shook her head again, more decisively.

'You're so tired you can't see straight,' she said with some justice. 'And I'm not a child any more.'

Paula pushed a distracted hand through her drying hair.

'I know you're not. But you're not in Eduardo Mascherini's league,' she said almost to herself.

Trish gave a small, unhappy smile. 'Are you?' she asked, her doubts showing.

Paula jumped. Then her gaze came back to the pale pointed face in front of her. Trish was holding on to her composure bravely but she was only twenty-one. She had no one to turn to but an elder sister who was out of the country when she needed her.

Paula showed her teeth. 'Oh, yes. I can handle him.'

'But you said...'

'When I'm angry,' Paula said calmly, 'I'm a match for the devil himself. Ask anyone in the office.'

Trish looked startled and even rather worried. Paula hugged her.

'Mascherini made me as angry as I can remember,' she explained. 'He's going to pay. I shall enjoy making him pay.'

'Oh, dear,' said Trish with feeling. She gave her sister a doubtful look. Paula's temper was seldom roused. She had been a rock-steady support after their mother died, unfailingly domestic and efficient, unfailingly patient with their increasingly erratic father. She dealt with problems without fuss; and she didn't—normally—pick fights.

But she had a strong sense of justice. Trish remembered a spectacular row with their father when Paula had discovered he had been diverting Trish's trust fund money.

She said uneasily, 'You won't go stirring things up, will you, Paula?'

'It looks to me as if they're already about as stirred up as they can get,' Paula replied with a dry look.

'Yes, but... I mean, I still haven't talked to Franco. Maybe he...'

Paula took her sister's hand.

'You left messages for him?'

Trish nodded.

'And told him how he could get hold of you?'

Trish bit her lip. Paula squeezed her fingers.

'Face it, pet, he's running scared. He's delegated it to the hit squad. So——'

'So you think I should do the same?' Trish interrupted.

Paula stared at her. Her gentle sister sounded almost angry.

'Paula, I *know* Franco,' she said earnestly. 'He wouldn't let me down. I know.'

Paula looked at her very steadily. Trish's eyes fell.

'I thought he loved me,' she said almost inaudibly. 'I can't believe he'd let me down.'

Paula's honesty fought with compassion; and lost.

'Maybe he won't,' she said cravenly.

She found her head was reeling, not unpleasantly. It was a symptom she recognised. If she didn't lie down and sleep soon, she would slide gently to the carpet and stay there. She made for the bedroom.

'Look, I'm dead on my feet, Trish. Stay here if you want,' she said over her shoulder. 'It'll be easier to phone from here anyway, I imagine.' She added as an afterthought, 'There's money in the desk drawer if you want it. I'll see you at breakfast.'

But when she got up the next morning there was a note from Trish on the little pine table in the middle of the kitchen.

'Seeing Franco,' it said briefly. 'Be in touch.'

Paula turned it over. It had obviously been scrawled in a rush. There was no clue as to whether Trish had written it last night or this morning. Nor, she thought wryly, whether that last sentence was a promise or a command.

She started a pot of coffee, sighing. She knew she was over-protective of Trish. Sometimes it was very hard not to be. Her sister didn't seem to have any defences at all.

'You can't live other people's lives for them,' she said out loud. She said it again, more firmly. Then she laughed suddenly. 'You're a fraud, Paula Castle,' she told herself. 'You can't even convince yourself.'

But a brief survey of the flat demonstrated that Trish hadn't slept there in either of the spare rooms. And there wasn't the usual debris of her occupation in the study or the sitting-room. So if she had spent a sleepless night sitting up over her problems, she had done it elsewhere.

There was nothing for Paula to do but go back to her coffee and start planning her day.

She cleared her mail, dictating a few replies into a hand-held dictaphone. It was mostly work, though there were a couple of private business letters in there as well. At first she had been horrified at the thought of asking her secretary to type private correspondence. But as the job took over more and more of her private time, the distinction between the two blurred increasingly.

She packed her briefcase and consulted her watch. No time this morning for her usual exercise. Paula frowned. She had been postponing exercise more and more recently. She would have to readjust her schedule more carefully. Look at how crazily she had reacted to Eduardo Mascherini last night. That had to be, she told herself as she had not stopped doing since he'd finally walked away, the effects of over-tiredness and general physical debility.

'Fling a few weights around and you'll get him out of your mind,' Paula told her mirrored image.

She put up her hair into its usual neat pleat with less than her usual efficiency. It was extraordinary how vividly she remembered his fingers against the sensitive skin of neck under her fallen hair. She jabbed a long hairpin into her scalp and winced.

It wasn't going to happen again. Neither the falling hair nor that terrible feeling of vulnerability. She skewered the hair into place with a final thrust. She looked at her modest tray of cosmetics and decided against it. She didn't use much make-up anyway and for some reason this morning it was particularly important to face the world as she was.

It did not, she told herself, have anything to do with Eduardo Mascherini and those cool, dismissive eyes. Heavens, she wouldn't have wanted him to be anything other than dismissive. The thought of attracting someone with that degree of cynical expertise made her blood run cold.

She glared at herself in the mirror.

'He's absolutely not your type. And you're not his,' she told the image.

She leaned forward, examining herself critically. Did she look so much more tremulous than usual? She was reminded of her younger self: eyes wide and a little scared. And her mouth—she peered at it. Could it really look softer and fuller and...?

As if you've been kissed, some mischievous voice inside her said. For the first time in too long.

'Hell!' Paula said softly. 'I'm going to have to be very careful.'

If his cousin was anything like him, it wasn't surprising that sweet, unguarded Trish had fallen for him. Well, Paula wasn't going to let them ruin Trish's life; and she wasn't going to let them have any effect at all on her own.

She wouldn't see Mascherini again, she promised herself. She would write. On the partnership's official notepaper. That would show him she wasn't playing games.

And she would put him out of her mind.

She rode the Underground to work, summoning all her strength and proving singularly ineffective at getting rid of the disturbing image. By the time she got to work, she was in a controlled rage.

'Hi,' said her secretary, looking up from her computer screen as Paula walked in. 'New York looks good but there's an in-tray like the Tower of Pisa.'

'Good,' said Paula, baring her teeth. 'I'm in the mood to demolish it.'

Her secretary chuckled. Paula's energy was legendary.

'I'll call up reinforcements,' she said, picking up the phone.

Paula was as good as her word. In three hours she had got to the fine walnut inlay at the bottom of her in-box and there were two typists from the general pool at work-stations in the outer office. Sarah came in to take away the last folders and the tapes Paula had dictated.

She hesitated in the doorway. Paula got up restlessly.

'How long before that lot's typed?'

Sarah raised her eyes to heaven.

'All right, all right,' Paula said irritably. 'I just want to get on.'

'What you need,' said Sarah soothingly, 'is a good battle. Failing that, why don't you go and hit the gym? By the time you're out of overdrive, I'll have this and the rest ready to sign.'

Paula laughed reluctantly. 'You know me too well,' she complained. 'Oh, all right. I'll get out of your hair.'

She picked up her sports bag from the cloakroom. There had been an audible sigh of relief as she left the office which she had tried not to hear.

Am I becoming a beast to work for? she thought.

The gym was in a pleasant club, full of plants and tiled fountains. It was hugely expensive but Kit Marriott had decided to take out a group membership. As much as anything, Paula had thought cynically at the time, to show the older practices in the City that they were successful enough to afford it. And, of course, it was owned by the Isola Group. Isola were Kit's most treasured clients.

She changed and went through a brisk exercise routine. Three weeks jetting the Atlantic had slowed her down, she thought ruefully. And reduced her endurance.

Maybe that was why she had reacted so strongly to Eduardo Mascherini. It made her wince to remember how thoroughly he had blown her famous cool.

'Let's hope I don't have to see him again,' Paula told her reflection ruefully as she repinned her hair after her shower.

Sarah looked up when she got back to the office.

'Feeling better?'

'Don't you mean better tempered?' Paula was remorseful. 'I'm sorry I was a pain this morning.'

Sarah nodded, accepting the apology. She was curious. It wasn't like Paula. 'Got something on your mind?'

Paula gave a small, unhappy smile.

'If it were any other woman in the firm I'd guess man trouble,' Sarah told her frankly.

Paula shuddered.

'Thought not,' agreed Sarah, not without regret. 'Anything I can do?'

'Not unless you can cancel the last three weeks,' Paula said with a sigh.

Sarah's eyebrows climbed. 'Something went wrong in New York? But Marriott was jumping up and down rubbing his hands with glee, I thought.'

'Something went wrong here while I was in New York,' Paula corrected quietly. 'Disastrously wrong. And I don't know what to do about it.'

Sarah was silenced. She had never heard Paula say she didn't know what to do before.

Paula shifted her shoulders impatiently.

'I'm not going to start thinking about it again. There's no point giving myself hell in the gym if I start winding myself up again the moment I get back. Bring those letters in and we'll polish them off.'

Sarah did. Paula ran her eyes down immaculately typed letter after letter. She signed each one and gave it back. Sarah took the folder and replaced it with another. Its contents were equally impeccable. Paula signed them all.

'There,' she said at last, sitting back with a sigh. 'That's the worst done.'

Sarah grinned at her. 'No, it isn't. Don't forget the bills.'

Paula groaned. 'Sadist. You're fired,' she said. 'You know me too well.'

'No, I'm not,' said Sarah. 'You know *me* too well. You'd never break in another secretary. Take your frustration out on the calculator.'

She drew the door to behind her with her foot. Paula pulled the blank time sheets towards her, muttering.

One of the things she hated most was sorting out the time for which she needed to charge her clients. Normally she did it every day but in the course of a long negotiation the discipline was abandoned. Now she would have to work out chargeable time for the last month.

She extracted a calculator from a drawer and set grimly to work. She was still going through neat columns of figures, wondering whether she really had managed to work through thirty-eight hours without a break even for sleep, when the intercom buzzed.

'Sarah,' she said dangerously, 'you know I can't add and answer the telephone at the same time.'

'I know but I think it's urgent,' Sarah said candidly.

'What is?'

'Marriott's been on.' Sarah didn't like the senior partner. 'There's an Isola meeting and he wants you to join them.'

Paula looked at the phone blankly.

'Isola?'

The international conglomerate's business had been the backbone of the practice since Kit Marriott first set up on his own. He never allowed any of his partners near his prime client.

'That's what I thought,' Sarah agreed with the unspoken comment. 'He didn't sound best pleased either. They must be looking at a really fiendish acquisition, if Marriott's admitting he's out of his depth.'

'Thank you for that encouraging thought,' Paula said drily. She stood up. 'Where is it?'

Sarah told her. Paula shrugged herself back into her severe jacket, flicked the collar of her blouse, so that its pearly lapels overlay those of the coat, and left her office with speed.

She didn't race into the meeting-room, though. No matter how she might sprint through the office, the clients always saw her measured and composed. At least they always had until now.

She walked in, started to say, 'You wanted a word, Kit?' and stopped dead.

Eduardo Mascherini, devastating in a dark, waistcoated suit of exquisite cut, was standing by the window. Kit Marriott was there as well but she hardly noticed him.

'What are you doing here?' Paula demanded.

Mascherini looked amused. 'It is delightful to see you again, Miss Castle.'

She swung round on Kit. 'What is this man doing here?'

Kit was wearing a fixed smile and a steely look about the jaw which was anything but sympathetic.

'Paula, let me introduce the Conte Bianche e Mascherini della Isola. Eduardo, Miss Castle, our international corporate specialist. As I promised.'

Paula took hold of the only word that made sense. 'Isola?' She felt as if she had been turned to stone.

'Delighted,' Mascherini murmured as he bowed ceremoniously over her hand.

Paula came abruptly back to life. She snatched her hand away as if the man had bitten her.

She encountered a look from Kit which explained her secretary's dislike of him. How could men manage to bully you without opening their mouths? Paula thought. Or try to. Paula herself didn't bully so easily these days. She gave him a bland smile.

'You should have told me you were a client of Marriott's, Conte,' she said sweetly. 'I wouldn't have been so alarmed when we—er—met.'

Mascherini looked amused. 'I wouldn't have said you were alarmed, Miss Castle. You must be the coolest woman I've ever met.'

Paula decided to take that as a compliment. She inclined her head.

'Thank you.'

The grey eyes danced.

'I see why Kit speaks so highly of you,' he murmured.

The briefest glance at Kit Marriott, who was curbing his annoyance with difficulty, made it obvious that he had not spoken of her at all. In spite of herself, Paula's lips twitched in answering laughter. She suppressed it.

'I'm flattered,' she said.

Kit was nothing if not smooth. He said easily, 'Eduardo's thinking about a rather tricky cross-border deal. It isn't even at the feasibility-study stage yet. He thought—that is, I suggested that you could help him put a price on the legal implications.'

Paula looked from one to the other thoughtfully. She had known Kit Marriott a long time. Smooth though he was, he could not hide it from her when he was being devious. On this occasion she was almost sure that he knew no more than he was saying. Mascherini, or whatever his name was, had simply taken the acquisition story to Kit. He had not hinted that there was anything personal between Paula and himself.

Not that there was, of course, she reminded herself quickly. The personal issues were between Trish and the elusive Franco.

She sat down at the polished boardroom table and gave Eduardo Mascherini a professional smile. She pulled one of the notepads from the middle of the table towards her and extracted her fountain pen from her top pocket.

'Where, when and who?' she asked.

There was a flash of something like surprise on that mocking face. She saw it with a certain satisfaction. Did he think she was going to throw up her hands in maidenly hysterics and refuse to work for him? It was an entertaining thought.

She sent him a look of innocent enquiry, pen poised. 'It's still—er—very much on the drawing board.'

So he hadn't got his story prepared. Paula made a neat cross at the top of the virgin page.

'I will bear that in mind,' she assured him. And waited limpidly.

He looked at Kit.

'And ultra-confidential.'

Kit's annoyance didn't even show.

'You won't need me while you talk to Paula about things that may never happen,' he said easily. 'And my in-tray calls.'

Paula realised she had been outmanoeuvred by a master. Her brows twitched together. The last thing she wanted was to be left alone with him. He watched her with a good deal of comprehension.

'Miss Castle would be glad of some coffee, I think,' Mascherini observed.

She wondered briefly how the status-conscious senior partner liked being used as a waiter. But she need not have done. Isola was his most important client. He took it like a lamb.

'I'll send some in,' Kit Marriott said easily.

'Thank you,' murmured Mascherini.

The door closed gently behind Kit.

CHAPTER FOUR

EDUARDO MASCHERINI drew out the chair opposite and sat down, his elbows on the polished wood, his chin on his linked fingers. He was studying her with every appearance of interest. To her great annoyance, Paula's eyes fell.

She said hastily, 'Target company?'

The narrowed eyes laughed at her. 'Discretion, Miss Castle, discretion. Let us call it—Fortification.'

Paula was used to clients who used code names. Normally they told their legal advisers what the real names were, though. She ought to ask. But she wasn't going to press Eduardo Mascherini for any information he didn't want to give her. So she shrugged. And wrote it down.

'Where is it incorporated?'

'Oh, here. London.'

'Are you sure of that?' she pressed. 'Sometimes companies can be incorporated offshore even when their main trading activity is in the UK.'

His mouth quirked. If it weren't for the cynical lines, it would be a very attractive mouth.

'I'm sure.'

She shrugged again. 'Well, we can come back to that if we have to. What does it do?'

'Strategic advice,' he said so promptly that she was sure he had just made it up. Not only that he had just made it up but that he thought it was very entertaining.

But even knowing that he was laughing at some private joke at her expense wouldn't help her to challenge him. He was too important a client to Marriotts.

Paula set her teeth and wrote that down too.

'Who owns it now?'

'The management.'

She looked up, surprised. 'And will they be willing to sell? If they own their own company...'

'No,' he said calmly. 'Not willing at all.'

He was still laughing at his private joke. Paula put her pen down with a snap.

'Look, you must know as well as I do that a take-over like that is doomed to failure. If the management own it and they don't want you, you're finished, even if you managed to buy the company on paper. The people who are running it would just move on and start up again. I assume that it's the people you're after?'

'Very perceptive,' he said in a voice that meant the opposite.

Paula felt herself flushing. She leaned forward angrily.

'We seem to be wasting each other's time here, Conte...Conte...' She'd forgotten the man's damned title name, she realised in flash of fury.

He smiled at her.

'Eduardo. Please.'

'Signor Mascherini,' she said with restraint, 'my time is very expensive. I hope you are enjoying this.'

'Oh, I am,' he said affably.

She sat up very straight.

'I'm glad. Because, frankly, I don't think you have the slightest intention of taking over anything in this country or anywhere else.'

His shoulders shook slightly. But he said in a solemn voice, 'I hope you will always be frank with me, Miss Castle.'

Paula strove with her temper and won. But only just.

'Then do me the courtesy of being equally frank.'

The beautiful mouth curled wickedly. She was suddenly and startlingly reminded of a fourteenth-century portrait she had seen in Florence once. It was of one of the local nobles, surrounded by the trappings of his wealth and fawning courtiers. It was beautifully painted. The face was as handsome as it was haughty. But what had really struck Paula was the man's expression of derision as he looked at the crowd bowing before him.

And that was how Eduardo Mascherini looked: as if he had seen all the meanness and deception in the world and there was nothing left that surprised him. It startled and disturbed her.

He stood up. It took all her self-possession not to flinch away from him as he towered over her. She was absurdly grateful that the width of the boardroom table was between them.

'Very well, Miss Castle. Frankness. You shall have it. I want to talk to your sister.'

Paula stood up too, glaring. 'You've wasted my professional time for that?'

His mouth quirked into a slanted, scornful curve.

'I think your priorities need a bit of attention, Miss Castle,' he said quietly. 'Or is your sister negligible in your world view?'

Paula drew a long, calming breath.

'My feelings for my sister, Mr Mascherini, are my private affair. I don't expect to deal with my private affairs in the office.'

He watched her. 'That's reasonable,' he said at last. 'Have lunch with me, then.'

'No, thank you,' said Paula instantly. She didn't need to think about it.

'Ring your secretary and tell her we're going out. She can cancel whatever's in your diary.'

Paula was too taken aback by this piece of casual arrogance even to be angry. She said sweetly, 'And how would you feel if you were the client I was blowing away, Mr Mascherini?'

'I hope I would be flexible enough to understand that priorities sometimes have to change,' he said fluently.

'Well, I'm not that flexible. I have an odd habit of keeping my word,' Paula said with bite.

The grey eyes narrowed. 'Have you got anything in your diary for lunch?'

She hadn't as a matter of fact and she knew it. Sarah was under instructions to keep the diary as free as possible for the first two days after Paula came back from a trip.

He saw her eyes flicker and gave a soft laugh.

'You're pure hellcat, aren't you, Miss Castle? Wilful. Obstructive. Now why? I ask myself. Just to prove that you can? Or are you trying to put me in my place?' He gave a soundless laugh. 'Don't you think it would be wiser to co-operate?'

Paula felt herself go cold. It wasn't what he said so much as the look of absolute assurance on the handsome, cynical face.

'You're threatening me.'

'Merely pointing out the balance of interest,' he corrected coolly.

There was a silence. His look was a blatant challenge.

She said with composure, 'Do you think you could get Kit to sack me? If I don't put you in contact with Trish?'

His smile grew. It was not a nice smile.

'I am not a fool, Miss Castle. I know you are a full partner. Kit couldn't sack you, even if he wanted to.'

'Then . . .'

'But you are a partner who shares in the profits. Which might go down with a bump if I took my business away.'

Paula stared at him without speaking. It occurred to her that for an operator with an international reputation he was not going about achieving his objective in the most subtle way. But she was too angry to think about the implications of that.

'My sister, however, is not a partner in this firm,' she said with icy rage. She tore the page of notes off the writing pad and screwed it up. 'So this is all quite pointless.'

'Oh, I don't think so,' he said softly.

He strolled round the table to her. Paula stood her ground, measuring him.

'Don't look so militant, my dear. I'm sure we will come to some agreement in the end. Over lunch.'

She folded the notepad to her chest and glared at him. 'I don't each lunch.'

'Then you should,' he said imperturbably. 'It might sweeten your temper.'

Paula thought with a sudden pang of her snappishness at Sarah this morning. It was out of character. And it was due in large measure to the behaviour of this man who now had the gall to complain about it.

Her chin came up. 'Your absence would do that much more effectively,' she assured him.

His eyebrows flew up. 'Really? Are you telling me my simple presence disturbs you so much?' he asked, all polite incredulity.

Paula could hear the amusement simmering beneath the surface and set her teeth. She did her best to retrieve the damaging admission.

'When it interrupts my work, yes.'

'Then have lunch with me and come back to work afterwards.'

Their eyes locked. Meeting the implacable grey stare, she felt suddenly breathless.

'Forget it,' Paula said curtly.

She prepared to shoulder her way past him. He stopped her with one hand on her arm. She did flinch then. She couldn't help herself. The long fingers were astonishingly strong. Paula had never felt so threatened, she realised.

But she wasn't going to let him see that. She shook herself free. Turning, she met his look head-on.

'If you want advice on a take-over bid, then I'm at your disposal. Otherwise I can't help you.'

He studied her face for a long moment. He seemed surprised, she saw.

'You're very determined,' he said in an odd voice.

'Don't you expect your lawyers to be determined?' she flashed.

His laugh was rueful suddenly. 'You're right. Of course I do. It's just that I don't normally find my lawyers holding out on me.'

'Oh, stop this,' Paula said, losing the last of her composure. 'I'm not your lawyer. And I am never likely to be. Please don't tell me fairy-stories about UK take-overs. I'm not entirely a fool.'

He had not taken his eyes off her face. 'No,' he mused. 'Not a fool. Maybe too clever for your own good, I would guess. Sometimes anyway.' The wicked smile grew. 'And I think that at times you can be very blind, Miss Castle.'

And astoundingly, unforgivably, he touched the back of his fingers to her cheek.

Paula went rigid. In the anonymous quiet of the interview-room it was somehow more shocking even than last night's kiss. Then, at least, he had had the excuse of anger. He had thought she was playing games with him and he had been in a rage. He was not in a rage any longer.

Now there was no misunderstanding between them and the passion of anger had cooled. He was cool and amused and utterly in command. Which made the caress a calculated insult.

In a voice which shook with suppressed rage, Paula said, 'Since you know I can hardly retaliate, that's not a very chivalrous thing to do.'

His eyes gleamed.

'So retaliate. I promise I won't tell.'

She set her teeth, refusing to meet his eyes. She was not going to allow herself even to see the challenge there. It was amused and blatantly sexual.

He had no *right*, she thought. No right to say things like that or look at her like that. Or make her feel as if he touched her, just by letting his eyes rest on her softly flushed cheeks.

He laughed. When she didn't move, he took her hand, unclenched her fingers from the fist she was making and drew it down his own cheek. The touch of his shaven skin was electric.

Paula gave a little cry as if she had been wounded and hauled her hand away. She heard the sound as her palm connected with that smiling mouth before she even realised she was going to slap his face.

His eyes flickered. But he was still smiling. He caught the hand back and pressed a light kiss into the assaulting palm.

'I still won't tell,' he assured her, laughing.

Paula stood very still. She was appalled. Privately she did not know what had got into her. She had never behaved like that to a client before. Never to any man. Never got anywhere near it, no matter how obnoxious he was.

Even with Neil she had masked her feelings and behaved with restraint. Neil had hurt her appallingly and given her every reason for anger. But she had stayed cool and dignified, held on to her self-command, shed her tears in private—never even dreamed of lashing out. Yet this man ripped all that precious self-control away from her with just a touch.

I am out of my depth, she thought, disturbed.

She collected herself and drew a deep breath.

'Signor Mascherini,' she said very quietly, 'I apologise.'

His eyebrows flew up. He looked very wicked. And very handsome.

'Oh, don't apologise, *cara*,' he protested. 'It takes all the fun out of it.'

Paula could gladly have hit him again. Instead she drew another steadying breath.

'I don't find this *fun*.'

He looked amused. It was unforgivable.

'Don't you?'

'No, I don't. And neither would you if you cared half as much for your cousin as you say you do,' she retorted.

The dark brows twitched together. For a moment Paula had the feeling she had scored a hit. But then he was laughing again.

'I've learned to take my entertainment where I find it,' he said, watching her expression.

It got her on the raw; just as it was meant to do. Even though she knew she was being wound up, it seemed as if she couldn't help herself.

'I am not your entertainment,' Paula said between her teeth.

'I find it surprising too,' he said mildly, as if he were agreeing with something she had said.

There was a smouldering pause. Then, as if he were relenting, he gave a soft laugh.

'Look, I need to talk to your sister and so do you. I can find her easily enough if I have to, you know.'

'Then why don't you?' she flashed.

He sighed. 'Is she going to listen to me? Of course not. Especially if she's at all like her sister,' he added drily. 'I need you to get the truth out of her. If there really is a baby. And if there is——' His face darkened suddenly. 'Believe me, it's the worst reason on the world for getting married. I know. She must be made to see that. They could only be unhappy. Completely different backgrounds. A one-night stand. It's crazy.'

Paula thought of Trish's face as she said, 'Franco wouldn't let me down.' It was unbearable.

'Trish has already told me the truth,' she said in a voice like cracked ice. 'As your cousin does not appear to have done to you. It was not a one-night stand.'

He went suddenly still.

'What do you mean?'

'I mean the cousin you're trying to protect has lied to you,' she said with satisfaction.

'Or your sister lied to you,' he pointed out.

'Trish doesn't lie.'

He seemed to consider. Suddenly he frowned as if he'd thought of something. He looked at her speculatively and then gave a slow smile. With a return to his former tone, he said softly, 'All the more reason why I should see her as soon as possible and you should come with me. Then I can sort this mess out. You can forget all about it. And we...'

Paula glared at him. 'We?' she prompted sweetly.

His eyes gleamed. 'Can see how much entertainment we can offer each other,' he said with complete sang-froid. 'Which is what we ought to be doing now. Instead of squabbling about other people.'

Paula stared at him in disbelief. There was a faint ringing in her ears.

The man is propositioning me, she thought.

She shook her head a little to clear it. She was now well out into uncharted water and she knew it. She knew, none better, the minefield when attraction overlapped with business obligations. But her reaction to Neil's working-day hints and evasions had not prepared her for the sheer outrage that swept over her now.

'Don't look so scared,' he said with a kindness she found detestable in the circumstances. 'It's an awkward start. But that's going to make it all the more of a challenge.'

She stepped back. 'This isn't the start of anything,' she said with precision. 'And I most certainly do not find it a challenge.'

His mouth quirked. 'Well, I do.'

She shrugged. 'That is your privilege. I have nothing more to say. Goodbye, Mr Mascherini.'

The violence with which she wrenched the door open was more of a guide to her feelings than the even tone. His wry expression made it evident that he realised it.

He followed her into the corridor. 'Not goodbye.'

She went swiftly down the carpeted corridor. He strode at her shoulder. She could almost hear his amusement in the firm strides.

'Goodbye,' she repeated over her shoulder.

At the lift block she halted. The elegant receptionist looked up from her desk, not trying to hide her interest. Paula curbed her temper, holding out her hand.

'Goodbye,' she said again, more loudly.

He took her hand and held it. He looked down at her, his eyes dancing.

'I shall not give up hope,' he said—loudly enough to be overheard.

Paula refused to blush. She almost had to tear her hand away. She flexed her fingers, wincing a little. He was stronger than you would have thought.

'Don't sit by the phone,' she advised drily.

The receptionist's eyes widened to saucers.

He laughed. 'I'll ring you,' he said, quite as if they were friends.

The receptionist watched him go mistily. As the lift doors closed on him, she sighed.

'Gosh, he's gorgeous,' she said.

Paula sniffed.

The receptionist had been with the firm for a year. She knew Paula's reputation for immunity to the male sex. But this evidence of lack of natural feeling astonished her.

'Don't you think so, Miss Castle?' she said, puzzled.

'I think you should get on with your work,' Paula said.

This news of her renewed snappishness reached her office before she did. Sarah looked up over her glasses as Paula walked past her desk.

'Problems?'

'Why should there be problems?' Paula countered, flinging her notepad down on Sarah's desk as she made for her office. 'Get that typed before lunch, would you?'

Sarah picked it up. 'Please,' she murmured.

Paula stopped, her hand on the doorknob. 'What?'

Sarah smiled. 'Please. A small courtesy you can't afford to forget. Especially if I'm going to be your only ally round here.'

'What?'

'You've had a field day,' Sarah informed her affably. 'You've offended Kit, and Tracy on the desk and the firm's most important client. You can't afford to alienate me as well.'

'I never could afford to alienate you—you know too much about me,' Paula said calmly. But she went back to Sarah's desk. 'Besides being the best gossip in the office. How did you hear all this?'

'Tracy,' Sarah said with a grin. 'I'm only the second-best gossip.' She pushed her glasses up her nose. 'Is it true you froze out the Dreamboat?'

'What?'

'That's what everyone else calls him,' Sarah said unrepentantly. 'I haven't seen the man myself. But I gather women queue.' She surveyed Paula in amusement. 'And you told him not to sit by the phone.'

Paula jumped. 'Am I under surveillance, for God's sake?'

'Not you,' said Sarah. 'Him.'

Paula stared.

'Do you know he bought Argent Mining in thirty-six hours? He took over Ulysses Communication before anyone even knew it was on the market. That's the way he bought the *Courier* too—for sentimental reasons, he said. Sentimental, for heaven's sake. His grandfather used to be their Milan correspondent so he just stepped in when it got into difficulties. What sort of man spends that kind of money on sentiment? I tell you, this one is seriously rich.'

'And seriously well informed,' Paula said drily.

She knew the Isola Group's history well enough but it surprised her that Sarah did. Sarah didn't normally take much interest in the affairs of other people's clients. Her next remark explained it.

'Seriously gorgeous too. With not even an ex-wife on the payroll. It's enough to make a girl weep.' She looked at Paula hopefully. 'Are we going to work for him?'

'Not unless he can think up a better excuse than he has so far,' Paula said unwarily. She saw Sarah's startled expression and went on hurriedly, 'Anyway, how do you know he's seriously gorgeous? You said you hadn't seen him.'

Sarah sighed. 'I lunch with people who do. Do you know they change their coffee-breaks when he's coming in, just so they can see him?'

'You're joking,' Paula said. Sarah shook her head. 'Oh, honestly. Sometimes my fellow women make me despair.'

'It's human nature,' Sarah said tolerantly.

'Nonsense. It's sheer unbridled adolescence. I've no patience with it.'

Sarah raised her eyebrows. 'You don't fancy him?'

'Of course I don't,' said Paula heatedly.

'You wouldn't change a coffee-break for him?'

'Not in any circumstances.'

'So what am I supposed to say when he calls?' Sarah asked.

'He won't.'

Sarah pursed her lips.

'He won't,' Paula insisted.

'OK, OK, fine. He won't call. But on the outside chance that he does—what do you want me to do?'

Paula shuddered inexplicably. 'I don't want to talk to him,' she said sharply. 'Tell him anything you like but keep him out of my hair.'

Sarah smiled. There was something about that smile that made Paula defensive.

'I'm too busy with real work to mess about with his hypothetical deals,' she said with emphasis. 'If he's got a real deal with names and a timetable, I'll see him. Otherwise get rid of him.' She saw Sarah's amusement and added sweetly, 'Look on it as an initiative test. This is how you prove you're management material.'

She went into her office and closed the door smartly on her secretary's laughter.

CHAPTER FIVE

THE rest of the day went in a whirlwind. As soon as New York opened, the faxes began to fly. Sarah drafted in a permanent assistant from the pool of pre-university temporary staff. She and Paula had no time to exchange anything other than the briefest instructions about work.

So it was not until the end of the day that Sarah said, 'Your sister rang a couple of times.'

Paula was conscience-stricken. 'Damn,' she said, angry with herself.

'It's all right, I told her how busy you were,' Sarah said consolingly. 'She quite understood. She said she'd sort it out herself. Whatever it was,' she added hastily, as Paula's eyes darkened.

Paula flexed her tired shoulders. 'That I doubt,' she said sombrely. 'Did she say where she'd be?'

Sarah consulted her pad. 'At the flat. Or——' She flipped the pages over. 'No, she rang back. She didn't know when she was going to be back. She said she'd call you tonight.'

'Well, there's nothing I can do until she does, then,' Paula said fatalistically.

She put her papers into her briefcase and snapped it shut. She became aware that Sarah was regarding her with a glint of not very well disguised mischief.

'And the Dreamboat called. Several times.'

Paula spun the lock on her briefcase with concentration.

'I hope he was equally understanding,' she said in a neutral voice.

68

'He said he'd catch you at home,' Sarah reported, straight-faced.

Paula looked up sharply. 'There's no need to look like that. He has an apartment in my block.'

Sarah grinned. 'He owns your block. Kit did the conveyancing.'

Paula bit her lip. The block; as much of her professional time as he wanted to pay for; and damned nearly the partnership by his own account.

Why on earth hadn't she recognised him that first afternoon? His photograph had been in the papers often enough. Except the newspaper shots didn't catch the height—or the glitter like the point of a rapier in the grey eyes.

'He can't be there much. I've never seen him before.'

Sarah's eyes were bright with curiosity. 'It sounds as if you'll be seeing him more from now on.'

'If he thinks he's going to get free legal advice from me because we're neighbours, he can think again,' Paula said after a pause.

'It didn't sound as if it was legal advice he was after,' Sarah murmured.

Paula lifted her briefcase from the desk. 'A word of advice, Sarah.'

Sarah looked enquiring.

'You don't want to believe everything you're told. Especially not about professional dreamboats. Or,' she added as Sarah opened her mouth, 'by them.'

Sarah laughed. 'OK. His interest is professional. And you're not interested at all. I'll make a note of it.'

'Do that,' agreed Paula. 'Goodnight.'

At home Paula put down her briefcase and let her expensive coat slide off her shoulders on to the floor. She turned over the mail on the chest in the hall. It was the usual: business cards from car hire firms and home caterers; letters from decorators, offering references; a couple of bills; someone who wanted to clean her carpets; an incomprehensible note from Isabel in an excited hand. Nothing from Trish. And a sheet of thick ivory inlaid paper folded in four.

As soon as she saw it, Paula's heart sank. Not a bill or a circular, she decided, turning it over. Almost certainly hand-written. She could see the shadow of swooping black letters.

Not opening it, she trailed her coat through to the sitting-room. And stopped dead.

It was filled with flowers. Not just ordinary, thank-you-for-a-good-job sort of flowers either but the sort of thing that Paula vaguely imagined a film star might receive on an opening night. There were orchids and lilies and syringa along with trails of exotic-looking greenery that almost covered her modest bookshelves. The smell was overpowering.

The coat fell from her suddenly nerveless fingers. She looked round in bewilderment. Occasionally a grateful client had sent her a bouquet to the office. They usually came in bowls and were made up mainly of stiff carnations without a scent. No one had ever sent her flowers to her home before. Not even Neil when he'd been at his most attentive.

Behind her the phone began to ring. Paula didn't even try to answer it. On the fourth ring the answering machine cut in. Whoever it was didn't leave a message.

'I need a drink,' Paula said out loud.

She strode into the kitchen, screwing up the unwanted circulars as she went. Then she paused, as a thought struck her. Looking down, she saw Isabel's note with fresh eyes. This time the writing wasn't so impenetrable.

'No message with flowers,' it said. 'Eduard? brought them. PS The vases are his.'

Paula set her teeth. No message indeed. There was a message all right. He was going to treat her like some brainless floozy and see if it got her on the raw.

He could give all the hints he liked about being attracted to her, but Paula recognised his attentions for what they were; pure mischief. It amused him to make her angry.

She screwed Isabel's note up tight and lobbed it at the wall.

Well, it did get her on the raw, for all sorts of reasons that she didn't want to think about. But that didn't mean she was going to phone him up and rant about it. Nor was she going to say thank you.

There were even flowers in the kitchen, a long trail of various ivies from a basket on the shelf over the sink and a huge vase of lilies on the cooker. Paula glared at them. If she wanted to cook—which was a rare occurrence, though he wasn't to know that—her grills would presumably be lily-scented for the next week at least.

The phone rang again. She winced. But a quick glance at her watch told her that Trish might well have got home from wherever she was going. So it could be her sister.

She picked up the wall phone, speaking over the recorded message.

'Paula Castle.'

'Paula. Paula, it's me. It's all right. Everything's all right.' Trish spoke over the last of the message in a rush.

Paula gave a great sigh of relief. She held the phone away from her face so that Trish shouldn't hear it.

'I'm with Franco.'

That didn't sound so good. Not if he was still lying to his cousin about the nature of their relationship.

'Where?' said Paula practically. But Trish was too excited to listen.

'He's glad about the baby. He's *glad*, Paula. He isn't scared or anything. We're going to get married as soon as we can.'

Paula felt her original relief falter and die. Her heart sank like stone. Trish was gentle and generous and quite unstoppable when she decided to give her all. A man who sent his cousin to do his fighting for him didn't sound at all the sort of husband impulsive Trish needed.

'Marriage is a big step,' she temporised.

'He said at once, "We must get married." He doesn't have any doubts at all.' Trish's tone was blissful.

'Do you?' asked Paula swiftly.

But Trish wasn't listening. 'Wish me luck, Paula.'

'Trish, listen, you don't have to do this. I can support you. Take some time to think about it. It's your whole life...'

But the time Trish had paid for had run out. Paula was talking to mechanical pips.

She replaced the phone slowly.

'Damn,' she said aloud. 'Damn, damn, *damn*.'

She sank down on to the wickerwork rocking-chair. It was incongruous in the high-tech surroundings but it was supremely comforting.

Paula began to rock gently. Trish wasn't a child, she reminded herself. There was no reason for this cold clutch of fear round her heart. And yet... And yet...

Paula thought of their childhood. Normally she banished the memories. They were painful. And picking over old hurts got you nowhere, in her view. But now she opened the door deliberately, bracing herself.

The pictures flooded back: Trish, laughing, playing with the other children; then, all too suddenly, a bewildered schoolgirl, not understanding why her father wouldn't talk to her. He must have been too ashamed, thought Paula with hindsight, though she hadn't realised that at the time. She hadn't known that there should have been a trust fund for Trish. She had still been a schoolgirl herself then and she hadn't known anything about money.

She'd known about the drinking, though; and the black, sullen moods when all he wanted was to be alone. It had been in one of those moods that he had hit Trish. She had come back from school with a calendar she had made in class and wanted to show him. He had probably not even known who she was; just known that this was someone coming between his black self-pity and the whisky bottle.

Paula had heard Trish cry out. Remembering, she closed her eyes. Sometimes, in a bad dream, she still heard that cry. She had run into the sitting-room, to find Trish up against the wall, her hand clutched against her reddening cheek, terrified.

Paula had scooped her up. At six Trish had been a sturdy child but fury had lent her strength. Their father had quailed.

'If you ever lay a finger on her again, we're leaving,' Paula had told him, Trish's head pressed into her shoulder.

He had blustered. But he had believed her. And until he died, of heart and liver failure after a massive binge, he had remained in awe of that threat.

He had hated Paula for it, of course. And it had showed. Most of the time he'd ignored her. Sometimes he'd lashed out with a bitter tongue. Paula had never reacted. He had taken no more interest in Trish than he had before. But he hadn't hit her. And when he'd gone on one of his drinking jags, he'd locked himself in the sitting-room, away from both of them.

But Trish had forgiven him. Opening her eyes, Paula passed a weary hand through her hair. It was Paula who had donned armour and fought back. Paula who had decided not to gamble on affection any more. Right up to the day their father died, Trish had been sweet and loving and wanting to help him.

'No sense of self-preservation,' Paula muttered. 'And too much love for the human race. What on earth's going to happen to her?'

The phone rang again. Trish must have found some more coins. Paula reached up a hand and hooked it off the wall.

'Hello?'

'You're back,' said a voice she was beginning to know. He sounded amused and satisfied at the same time. As Paula stiffened he said, 'Your place or mine?'

'I don't know what you're talking about,' she said coldly.

'You need to thank me for the flowers. And I——'

'No, I don't,' she interrupted swiftly. 'I'm allergic to them and I can't find any of my books.'

He laughed. 'Lot of them, are there?'

'Flowers or books?'

'Flowers. I've already noticed your living-room could double as a library.' He sounded faintly disapproving.

'Why do you ask? Surely you know how many flowers you sent me?' she snapped, annoyed.

'No.' She could hear the grin in his voice. 'I just told Marietta to fill the place. She and your cleaning lady were in and out of here all afternoon, borrowing stuff.'

Paula said icily, 'Do I understand that you instructed a member of your staff to invade my home in my absence?'

'Your cleaning lady was there.' He didn't begin to sound repentant. 'Isabel, she said her name was. She was very helpful. I gather she's a bit of a romantic. She helped a lot.'

She would, thought Paula in silent fury. Isabel held strong views on the lack of men in Paula's life.

'Then I will give the flowers to her,' she said sweetly.

Eduardo Mascherini chuckled. 'You'll have to give her a pantechnicon to go with them.'

Paula gave up. The man had the hide of a rhinoceros.

'So as I said, your place or mine?'

'If you turn up here,' Paula said in a level voice, 'I give you fair warning I shall call the police and tell them you're harassing me.'

There was a little silence. That's stopped him, she thought with satisfaction.

Then he said softly, 'Coward.'

'I am not a coward.'

'Yes, you are. Why else are you trying to avoid me?'

'Because I'm tired,' Paula shouted down the phone, driven beyond endurance. 'Because I'm worried. Because I have hardly any free time and what I do have I want to spend relaxing.'

'Relax with me,' he suggested in a voice as smooth as cream.

'I'd as soon relax in a tiger's cage,' she muttered.

'My place, then.' She could hear the laugh in his voice.

'Don't you listen to anything anyone says to you? No.'

'And don't you want to know why you needn't worry about your sister any more?'

'No, I don't. I don't want anything to do with you.' She was shouting again when she suddenly registered the critical word. 'Sister?' she said in a more moderate tone.

'I told you I could find her without your help,' he said cheerfully. 'She wasn't as hostile as you,' he added.

'She is too trusting,' Paula said grimly.

'A lot more than you are, certainly. You know, I think it bears examining.'

'What does?'

'The difference. I would never have believed you were sisters, if you hadn't both told me you were.'

'You know us both so well, of course.'

'Trish is easy to know.' He paused deliberately. Paula set her teeth and refused to encourage him. 'And I have one or two theories about you that it might be rewarding to test,' he added in a caressing voice.

Paula felt as if she had been punched in the stomach. The innuendo was blatant. Had he no inhibitions at all? She pressed her free hand to her burning cheek, glad that he couldn't see her.

'Rewarding for whom?' she managed.

'Both of us, I hope. And your sister, of course.'

That gave Paula pause. Was he putting some sort of disreputable price on Trish's happiness? She thought of the joy in her sister's voice on the phone. Did he mean that he wouldn't interfere in her relationship with Franco as long as Paula did whatever he wanted?

'Are you talking blackmail again?' she said in a hard voice at last.

'If I have to.'

Paula's heart squeezed into a tight, hard knot.

'You mustn't.'

'I would prefer not to, of course. But——' She could imagine the shrug with which he finished the sentence. He sounded quite implacable.

'No. It's their business. You have no right to interfere.'

'That's an interesting point of view.' He paused. She heard the glimmer of laughter along the telephone line. 'Not one it's easy to discuss on the telephone. I think we should meet.'

Paula closed her eyes. She knew when she was defeated. She looked round the prima donna's bower he and his florist had made of her flat and decided she couldn't take any more invasion.

'I'll come up,' she said.

His flat was huge and decorated with the sort of pale furniture and glass that said, silently, that the owners weren't often there. Seating herself on a cream leather sofa, Paula took note. Anything was better than looking into those cynically amused eyes. Eduardo Mascherini hadn't been in any doubt at all that she would dance to his tune. In the end. Her being here simply proved what he had already known.

There were several sculptures, she noted a little desperately. They looked valuable. There were five or six shelves of books, nowhere near as many as she had, and a cabinet full of hand-painted china that looked old. He had managed to make the main room moderately untidy, with a scatter of books and papers, but there was no real disguising the fact that the apartment had never been anyone's home.

There was a brandy glass on a chunky glass table, and beside it a discarded file. The brandy looked untouched. He had obviously been stretched out on the sofa reading before he telephoned her. He looked as if he had made himself thoroughly comfortable.

He gave her a brandy without asking her what she wanted to drink. Paula took it. She had no intention of drinking it. Not on an empty stomach and not alone with Eduardo Mascherini.

She touched the glass to her lips without drinking and looked round.

'Do you look after yourself while you're in London?' she asked politely. She couldn't imagine this man wielding the dusters and polish the beautiful room demanded.

He looked down at her.

'If you're asking whether I'm domesticated, the answer is no,' he said calmly. 'If you want to know whether we're alone, then yes. I gave Bernardino the night off.'

'Oh.'

She thought it was a neutral enough sound but he sent her a glance of sudden annoyance.

'Weeks ago. He's gone to a concert.'

'Oh,' said Paula again. In a rather different tone.

'Before I even knew you existed. Much less started plotting your downfall,' Eduardo told her with a flash of teeth.

'*Oh*!' Her eyes flashed up to his, startled and confused.

'That's better,' he said with satisfaction. He dropped on to the sofa at right-angles to her own and leaned back among the maltreated cushions, watching her. 'You know, you're a real contradiction,' he told her.

She made a small gesture of rejection. 'I don't think so.'

'No, you wouldn't. I can see that. But you are.'

Paula set her teeth in a way that was becoming familiar in his company. She refused to ask in what way. That too was becoming familiar. Eduardo laughed.

'When I first met you I thought, That's a woman who knows what she wants. Tough as nails, maybe, but she knows where she's going.'

Paula winced. But, 'True enough,' she said coolly. She found his eyes uncomfortably penetrating.

'Ah, but it isn't, is it?'

She made a great business of picking up the brandy glass again.

'Of course it is.'

'No.' He sounded positive. 'If it were, we wouldn't be sitting here like this, fencing.'

Paula considered and hurriedly discarded the idea of asking him what he thought they would be doing instead.

'I don't think you know enough about me to make a judgement,' she said coolly.

'Maybe. I know a lot, though,' he told her softly. 'More than most people, I bet.'

She gave a little superstitious shiver. 'Don't be ridiculous,' she said, denying it. 'We've hardly met.'

'But I've seen you with your defences down,' he said. 'That puts me ahead of the game.'

Paula swallowed. 'You're imagining it.'

'No.' He was tranquil. 'No. You—interest me. So I asked. The people you work with think you're a robot. Even your secretary says you're programmed to put work first and pleasure a long way down the list. With emotion not figuring at all. Do you know that?'

'Yes,' said Paula, disguising her hurt. There was no reason why she should be hurt, after all. It was a fair enough statement of the way she chose to live her life. 'It's true.'

She found he was watching her with an odd smile.

'I've said before, you're blind, Miss Castle.'

She moved impatiently. 'I——'

'Of course I had an advantage,' he mused. 'I threatened your baby sister, didn't I?'

'You have an odd idea of an advantage,' Paula said drily.

He stretched lazily, clasping his hands behind his head.

'Well, it gave me sight of the emotion. Real emotion. You were ready to kill to protect her, weren't you?'

'I still am,' said Paula. 'And that's what we're supposed to be talking about.'

'No,' he said gently.

She stared at him. 'I came here to talk about my sister and her future, such as it is, if she stays with your cousin.'

'You came because I invited you,' he corrected. 'And I invited you because I want to talk about you. Not your sister or Franco. You.'

Paula said, 'Then you got me here on false pretences.' She stood up.

'Sit down,' he said lazily.

She stood her ground.

'I think Kit Marriott's obedience must have gone to your head, Mr Mascherini,' she said cordially. 'We're not in the office now. You can't tell me what to do.'

He laughed up at her.

'That doesn't sound much like a robot to me.'

Paula bit her lip.

'In fact it sounds like a woman who lets her heart rule her head. *And* speaks before she thinks. A passionate, impulsive woman who doesn't plan her every move.'

She looked at him bitterly. 'Is that what you like? A woman out of her own control? Is that what you want?'

His brows twitched together. His eyes were shrewd. But he said equably, 'If you're asking whether I want you, then you must know the answer is yes.'

Paula gasped. Even for a man with no inhibitions, it was outrageous. And it was the last thing she expected him—or anyone—to say. She had no answer prepared. She floundered, horridly aware of an uncontrollable blush.

He gave a soft laugh. 'Don't look so astonished. I've wanted you almost from the first moment we met. And you know it.'

'No,' she said in a stifled voice.

'Oh, yes. And you want me too. The only difference between us is I'm prepared to admit it.'

'You're crazy,' Paula said with conviction.

He grinned. 'My best friends would agree with you. This is quite out of character for me.'

'I'm glad to hear it. Or you'd have been locked up.'

'Rude,' he said appreciatively. 'New situations call for new tactics. I've never been in this situation before.'

'Neither,' said Paula rather grimly, 'have I. Mr Mascherini...'

'Eduardo,' he corrected her.

She sent him a look which in the past had stopped international corporate lawyers at twenty paces. It had no noticeable effect on the lounging figure on the couch.

'Mr Mascherini, I am here because you said—implied—that you had it in your power to start bullying my sister. I want to know what you're going to do.'

He surveyed her thoughtfully. 'Jumps to conclusions,' he murmured. As if, Paula thought, he were dictating a file note on her. 'Probably only when strongly moved, however.'

She stood there, her hands balling into fists by her side. She felt herself hating him so much it must show, like a rash.

'*Tell* me,' she said. To her consternation her voice broke on the last word.

He swung his legs round and stood up in one swift, lithe movement. He towered over her, so close that she could see a dusting of silver at his temples; too close.

'Sit down,' he said. Gently this time.

Paula sank bonelessly back on to the sofa. He hunkered down in front of her, his gaze searching.

'You love her very much, don't you?'

She closed her eyes briefly. 'Of course I do. She's my sister.'

He picked up the untouched brandy glass and sat down on the sofa beside her.

'My sister and I don't give a damn about each other,' he said idly.

Her eyes flew open. He held out the glass.

'Drink it. You look as if you need it.'

There was no arguing with that, Paula thought wryly. She had probably never been more in need of a strong pick-me-up in her life. She took a sip of the fiery stuff, grimacing as it hit the back of her throat. She didn't drink much and she didn't like spirits. But there were some things it was worth fighting Eduardo Mascherini about and some where it was just easier to give in.

'Is she your only sister?'

Paula nodded.

'What about the rest of the family?'

Paula shrugged. 'There never was much of a family. Grandparents were all dead before I was born. Then my mother died. My father limped along for a bit. They were both only children. That left Trish and me when he died.'

'How old were you?'

'Eighteen,' said Paula without thinking. Then suspiciously, 'Why do you want to know?'

He put out a hand and picked up a stray frond of hair from behind her ear.

'Hmm? Oh, I want to know everything about you.'

Paula shuddered. It was too reminiscent of Neil, that. She'd been there. She moved away from him.

'And how do you feel about being known?' she demanded edgily.

'I'll tell you anything you want to know,' he said with the promptness of a man who'd been hoping she would ask exactly that question.

Paula ignored the mischievous invitation in the grey eyes. She turned and looked him straight in the face, her expression serious.

'Then tell me what you're going to do about my sister.'

He shrugged. 'I've put her in touch with Franco. After that they're on their own.'

'*What*?'

'You impressed me, you see,' he said, a small smile curling the corners of his mouth. 'You said so firmly that it was their own business, even though you were clearly worried sick. I thought, If she can take that attitude, so can I.'

Paula stared at him. 'Then what am I doing here?'

He sighed. 'Doesn't listen,' he murmured. 'To talk about us, dearest Miss Castle. You and me. And see what we do about what we feel for each other.'

'We—I—don't——'

He flung up a hand. 'Don't tell me you don't feel anything for me. You were hating me so badly back there it was coming off you in waves.'

Paula had to admit that he was right. For the first time she smiled reluctantly. 'I'd have thought the cure for that was not to see each other again,' she said drily.

He watched her as if fascinated.

'No. That just puts it on ice. Very unpredictable, ice.'

'Then what is the cure?'

There was a strange, measuring look in his eyes. Paula had a sudden, unwelcome feeling that he had summed her up and was manipulating her like a master.

He said slowly, 'Do you want a cure?'

Paula dragged her eyes away from his. 'I would like to be left in peace to get on with my life,' she said with more firmness than she was feeling.

His eyes narrowed. She had the feeling he was debating whether to touch her. She tensed. But he didn't. Instead he said, 'Peace. Yes. I can relate to that. All right. Let's negotiate.'

Startled, Paula looked into his eyes again. It was a mistake. She couldn't read their expression at all. They were also mesmerising.

'Negotiate?'

'I understood that's your forte.'

'Well, yes,' she agreed, taken aback. 'But not normally in my personal life.'

'That,' he told her, 'is obvious. So start here. You want me out of your hair. I want the reverse.' His eyes skimmed the blonde pleat, fraying after a hard day, and Paula felt her cheeks warm again. 'So let's have some ground rules.' He leaned forward. 'I assume there've been men in the past—a beautiful woman like you.'

Paula glared at him. 'Of course,' she said grandly.

It wasn't strictly true unless you counted Neil. But you had to count Neil, she thought wryly, because he was the reason there hadn't been anyone since.

'But no one now?'

'I haven't the time.'

'Or recently.'

She hadn't seen Neil for eight years. 'No,' she agreed reluctantly.

His eyes flickered.

'Did you live with him?'

Paula thought of Neil's furtive visits to her small apartment. He hadn't wanted their colleagues to find out, of course. Though she hadn't realised that at the time. At the time she had just been hurt and bewildered.

'No,' she said curtly.

'Love him?'

She had loved Neil. Well, she must have done or his weak-kneed betrayal wouldn't have hurt so much. But she wasn't admitting that to Eduardo Mascherini.

Paula looked away, shrugging.

'So,' he said, ticking the points off on his fingers as he summed them up, 'no commitment at the moment; no broken heart; no shadows from the past. What have you got to lose?'

'In doing what?' asked Paula. Though she knew, of course.

He grinned at her. 'In having an affair with me.'

She looked into his laughing eyes and felt something stir inside her. It was unfamiliar and rather alarming. She closed down the feeling as if she were slamming a lid on a boiling pot.

'My time,' she said crisply. 'I don't have time for an affair. To say nothing of my self-respect, my professional reputation and my currently unbroken heart. Does that answer the question?'

His expression was almost tender.

'Do you think I'd hurt you?'

Almost certainly, thought Paula, thinking of Neil. She didn't say that, however.

'I haven't got the spare capacity in my life to be able to afford the time to find out,' she said carefully.

'But if you don't find out, you'll always wonder,' he pointed out. 'Now that's a real waste of time.'

She glared at him. He met her look limpidly. At last she sighed, torn between impatience and a reluctant respect for his persistence. She could see why he was a successful businessman, she thought.

'This is crazy. You can't just set out a proposal to have an affair like a—a take-over prospectus,' she expostulated.

'So draw me up an alternative,' he returned. 'One that you'd find acceptable.'

Paula closed her eyes in exasperation. 'What do I have to do to convince you?' she said. 'I don't want to have an affair with you.'

He laughed. 'I'm convinced.'

She was bewildered. 'Well, then . . .'

He touched her face very gently. 'There's wanting to. And needing to. Having to. This isn't what you'd have chosen, I can see that. Nor I, to be honest. Only it's happened and we can't walk away from it.'

Paula searched his face and found that he was serious. For some reason she found that alarming. She scrambled to her feet.

'Nothing's happened,' she said in a high, breathless voice.

Eduardo Mascherini stood up more slowly and a great deal more gracefully. He was smiling.

'Oh, yes, it has.'

Paula looked into dark grey eyes that were so intent they were almost black. She thought, He's going to kiss me again; another old-fashioned sweeping off the feet that's supposed to make me wilt at his strength.

She took a step backwards. She was shaking with rage. Or she assured herself it was rage.

'No, it hasn't,' she said firmly. 'And what's more it isn't going to.'

He laughed.

She flung her head back. 'It *isn't*,' she insisted. 'I am in control of my life and I can tell you this is where your little game stops. Here and now.'

He shook his head; mock-sorrowfully, she thought.

'It's not little. It's not a game. And nobody in the world is in control of his life. Haven't you learned that yet?'

Paula drew a deep breath. 'I did not come here for a lecture on your philosophy of life.'

'Another time,' he murmured, amused.

She ignored him. 'This nonsense has got to stop now. If you persist in hounding me, I'll—I'll——'

He was very close, she suddenly realised.

'It isn't me that's hounding you,' he said.

She stared at him, stumbling into silence. He drew his thumb very lightly across her lower lip. She felt as if someone had run a sunlamp up her spine. She gasped.

'Yes,' he said as if he were agreeing with her. 'You and me both, darling. But have it your way.' He shrugged. 'I won't come to you until you come to me.'

Paula swallowed, shaken. I won't, she vowed. I won't. And I won't give him the satisfaction of contradicting me, either.

He smiled at her, as if he knew what she was thinking. 'Just don't make it too long,' he said.

CHAPTER SIX

IT WAS impossible to get rid of the things Eduardo Mascherini had said, Paula found. They cost her a sleepless night. And they haunted her through the following day.

Of course, it was easy enough to forget him while she was working. But it was astonishing the amount of time that Paula discovered that she didn't work: when she was waiting for someone to answer the phone, for example; or when she repaired her make-up before a meeting. She suddenly found herself staring into the mirror, the lipstick wand idle between her fingers, and hearing the man saying, 'Just don't make it too long.'

She met her own eyes in the mirror. They were wide and the colour of storm clouds, instead of their usual clear grey. Not much self-possession there. It was unnerving. It was a long time since she had lost sleep over a man, Paula thought wryly.

It meant that when Trish arrived with Franco Paula was almost shocked, bounced out of her preoccupations by the ringing of the doorbell.

She flung open the door as if to see off the devil himself. She was taken aback to see Trish in the doorway, her arm through that of a man Paula had never seen before.

'This is Franco,' said Trish radiantly, surging in while Paula was still collecting herself. 'Franco, darling, my wonderful sister Paula.'

Paula took hold of herself and held out her hand. 'How do you do? It's nice to meet you at last,' she said drily.

Trish sent her a quick, minatory look. But Franco seemed unaware of the disapproval.

He bowed over the hand. 'Franco Gratz,' he said. 'I believe you have met my cousin.'

'Indeed I have,' said Paula.

Trish pulled him into the flat with another warning look at Paula. She led the way into the sitting-room and flung herself down on the rug, spreading her hands at the flames in the grate.

'It's freezing out there. You'd never think it was spring. I'm so glad you've got the fire on, Paula. Franco stayed in Eduardo's flat the first time he was here and it's *icy* up there.'

'I didn't notice...' said Paula unwarily.

She found two pairs of eyes regarding her in open astonishment.

'You mean you've been up there? Bearded the lion in his den?' said Trish.

Paula felt herself blushing faintly and was annoyed.

'Don't be ridiculous,' she said more sharply than she intended. 'We had a perfectly civilised discussion.' Paula thought about it. 'Well, we agreed that it was your business and we weren't going to interfere,' she corrected conscientiously.

There was no point in telling them about Eduardo's uncivilised and highly questionable behaviour in matters that didn't concern them.

'You are a miracle worker,' Franco assured her fervently. 'My cousin Eduardo thinks everything is his business. At least as far as family is concerned. And he has spies everywhere.'

Paula thought this a little highly coloured. Her expression must have given her away because Trish chimed in, 'Oh, he *does*, Paula. He's the most dictatorial, determined man. You've no idea.'

Have I not? thought Paula. But all she said was, 'Well, sit down, Franco, and tell me what you and Trish have decided to do.'

She did her best to sound neutral. From the look Trish gave her she wasn't sure she succeeded. Franco didn't seem to notice anything wrong, though.

He sat down on the edge of a chair. He was not very like his cousin, she saw. He was handsome enough, but his face lacked that harsh, sculpted look; and his eyes, she saw with a slight start of surprise, were kind. He didn't look like the playboy seducer she had imagined.

Trish looked up at him and smiled. Instinctively, it seemed, their hands met. It was eloquent. Suddenly feeling very alone, Paula looked away. Her reaction startled her. Was it envy?

'We will marry,' Franco said positively. He smiled down at Trish. 'I wanted to anyway. But I thought it was too early to ask. Now—Trish has agreed and I have told my mother.'

His mouth firmed. Paula detected an unspoken issue. She looked from one to the other in enquiry. Her sister smiled comprehendingly. She gave Franco's hand a little tug.

He sighed. 'I must tell you something about my family, Paula. It is not quite as medieval as it seems. But there has been a lot of family ill will in the past. And when there are family companies involved, that can be disastrous.'

Paula tried to remember what she had ever known about the Isola Group. She frowned. Was there something about a successor to the top job whom no one expected?

Franco spread his hands. 'Ours is not a united family.' He hesitated. Then he shrugged. 'You are our London lawyers. Maybe you know this?'

Paula shook her head.

'Well, my grandfather was a tyrant. My uncle Leo married Eduardo's mother in secret. Then my grand-father wanted him to marry an heiress and he went through another form of marriage. It wasn't legal, of course. They had a daughter. He still went to see his first wife, who didn't know anything about it. When he died the inheritance complications were appalling. Eduardo says it must never happen again. The company couldn't stand it.'

Her eyes narrowed. 'No one expected him to inherit?'

'No one knew he existed.' Franco sounded strained. He looked apologetic. 'I'm sorry. This must sound crazy. But I was only a child then and I still remember how for months the house was full of screaming women who thought they or their offspring had been cheated. Well, my mother was one of them. I often wondered if that was why——' He broke off abruptly.

'Why?' Trish prompted.

He shrugged. 'Why Eduardo is such a bastard to his women. He was only twenty-five and they gave him a bad time.'

Paula stored that away for her further information. A bastard to his women, was he? Well, that was no more than her own instincts were already warning her. Interesting to have it confirmed, though.

But Trish had no interest in Cousin Eduardo.

'Go on,' she said impatiently. 'Tell her about your mother.'

Franco looked faintly unhappy. 'She was the baby of the family. They adopted her when she was small. She was spoilt, I suppose. Anyway, she always felt she was closest to my grandfather. She married his right-hand man. She expected to inherit. When I was born, she expected me to inherit. And then—out of the blue—my grandfather's lawyers said there was an heir. A legitimate, male, direct descendant.' His mouth twisted at the memory.

'It was fifteen years ago,' he said quietly. 'I can still remember the screams.'

'But why?' Paula was intrigued. 'Why did no one know?'

'My uncle Leo was a strange man. He was like an adolescent. He hated my grandfather telling him what to do. But he didn't have the courage to break away. He married Eduardo's mother when he was on a business trip. And he just kept going back to visit her. He had a complete double life. She didn't know he was rich. She didn't know about the title. She thought he was a travelling salesman. So of course, when he died, nobody knew that she ought to have been told. When he didn't come back, Eduardo started to look for him. By then my grandfather was ill.' Again Franco shrugged. 'He died before he could change his will properly. But he left a declaration in front of witnesses that Eduardo was to have everything. And he'd already put Eduardo on the board. When he died, all the aunts sued. It went on for years. It cost the company a fortune. And as for Eduardo—who knows what it cost him?'

Paula said slowly, 'I don't see what this has to do with you and Trish.'

Franco was earnest. 'I want you to understand, Paula. My family has been torn apart once already by an unsuitable marriage in a distant city. Eduardo wanted to make sure that it didn't happen again.'

Paula kept to herself the impression that Eduardo had wanted to make sure that it didn't happen at all.

'Understandable,' she said in a neutral voice. 'So why didn't he contact you, instead of trying to intimidate Trish?'

And me, she thought. And me, oh, God.

Franco looked even more uncomfortable. But Trish was more robust.

'Oh, that was because he got the wrong end of the stick entirely,' she assured Paula sunnily. 'That woman I told you about. The glamorous one. She told him that I was a gold-digger and had trapped Franco after a one-night stand.'

Paula's brows knitted. 'He told me *you'd* told him that,' she told Franco. Try as she would, she couldn't keep the contempt out of her voice.

Trish was indignant but Franco said quietly, 'That's what he believed. He knows better now.'

'But why?'

He shifted his shoulders. 'When Trish went to the flat Eduardo wasn't there. But a—friend of the family was. Gina Pesce.'

'I told you,' Trish reminded Paula, 'terribly glamorous. She scared me stiff.'

Franco reached out and took her hand firmly in his.

'She told Eduardo, of course. But first she told my mother. They—they seem to have convinced themselves that there was some sort of blackmail attempt going on. Eduardo told me some silly story about diamonds and compromising photographs. When I said that Trish and I loved each other, he was perfectly reasonable.'

'Why did he listen to this woman rather than talk to you in the first place?' said Paula suspiciously.

'Gina? Well, they have been friends a long time.' He paused, frowning. 'My mother thinks they will marry. But I don't know. I don't think Eduardo will marry anyone.'

'They travel together?'

Franco looked amused. 'Eduardo travels alone. But Gina has the use of the flat when she's in London. I suppose they just coincided this time.'

'And she prevented you from speaking to each other?' Paula asked in disbelief.

'You have to understand, Paula. I was in Khirgistan on business. There is a telephone system but you have to wait. You never know when your calls will come through. I never managed to connect with Eduardo. Well, he is so busy, it's not surprising. I left messages with Gina. She must have misunderstood what I was saying. The lines were awful.'

Paula looked at her sister. It sounded thin to her. Why hadn't he called Trish rather than his cousin?

But Trish was unconcerned. She said cheerfully, 'It doesn't matter. We found each other in the end.'

'Yes,' Franco said softly. He smiled at her with tenderness.

For all her doubts, Paula felt a sudden sharp exclusion from their closeness.

'I'm very glad for you,' she said briskly, to disguise it. 'What happens next?'

They began to tell her about their wedding plans. It was clear there was one cloud on the horizon.

'Franco's mother says she won't come,' Trish confessed. Her lower lip trembled.

Paula made to put her arm round her. But Franco drew Trish against his shoulder, smoothing the hair off her brow with a loving hand. Paula's arm fell.

He said quietly, 'Eduardo could persuade her.' He looked at Paula.

Paula said composedly, 'Then you'd better ask him to do so, hadn't you?'

Franco looked uncomfortable. 'He always says he doesn't get involved in female disputes.'

'He was ready enough to get involved in your private life,' Paula pointed out drily.

'That's because it might lead to difficulties of inheritance. Eduardo cares about the company. Only the company. He doesn't care about the family at all. Sometimes I think he doesn't care about people.'

Paula remembered him saying thoughtfully, 'My sister and I don't give a damn about each other.'

Trish said eagerly, 'But he respects you, Paula. He really does. He said I was lucky to have a sister who stood up for me. If you asked him . . .'

'No,' said Paula.

Trish didn't appear to hear. She said thoughtfully, 'He seemed very interested in you. He asked a lot about you: what you did, whom you went out with.'

Paula met her sister's eyes. They were limpid blue and innocent. But she read the message there. Trish wasn't above blackmail either when she thought something was really important. Ask him to persuade Franco's mother to come and I won't tell him about Neil, Paula read, as clearly as if Trish had written it on a sign and held it up.

Franco was oblivious. 'Would you, Paula? Perhaps if you and he went to see my mother together . . .' A sudden mischievous light came into his eyes '. . . she would see I wasn't marrying into a family of saloon girls.'

Paula thought of going anywhere with Eduardo Mascherini and her throat closed.

'I'm busy,' she said. She looked at Trish. 'You know.'

'Well, maybe if you just convince Eduardo to get involved,' Franco urged.

Paula looked at Trish and sighed. 'Very well.'

Trish hugged her. Franco gave her the phone. He even dialled the number for her.

The manservant answered. She asked for Eduardo in her best lawyer's clipped tones.

The Count, she was told, was not in. He would be sorry to have missed Miss Castle.

Paula, who had deliberately not given her name, flushed. Franco's eyebrows went up.

He was at the opera, a long-standing engagement. He would no doubt wish to return her call tonight although he might be very late. Up to what hour would it be convenient for Miss Castle to receive his call?

It was a temptation to say she would be going to bed early. But then it would only have to be done tomorrow. Paula knew that putting things off only made them worse.

'Oh, any time,' she said. 'I've got a lot of work. I won't be going to bed early.'

'I will tell the Count. Goodbye, Miss Castle.'

She relayed the substance of the conversation to Trish and Franco. Trish looked disappointed.

'We'll stay till he calls,' she said.

Franco looked amused. 'We can't do that, darling. He might not call.'

'But that man said he'd ask him to call when he got back,' she protested.

He laughed. 'He might have better things to do. Especially if he's gone with Gina. She wouldn't be pleased if he wanted to telephone another woman.'

Trish digested this. She looked put out. Franco hugged her.

Paula said reassuringly, 'I'll tell you as soon as I've talked to him.'

'Oh, all right.' Trish leaned against Franco, telling him, 'You'd better take me somewhere and feed me. I haven't eaten enough for one today, let alone two.'

'At once,' he said, kissing her lightly.

Once again, Paula felt that little shiver of exclusion. She fought it down.

They said an affectionate goodbye. But it was obvious that they didn't really have much attention left for anyone but each other. It was natural, of course, she reminded herself. But it made her feel lonelier than she had felt for a long time.

She prowled the flat restlessly. She couldn't settle to work, though there was a pile of it in her briefcase.

She took a detective novel off the shelves. But she had to push a trail of jasmine and ivy out of the way to get at it and it brought Eduardo as vividly to mind as if it were his hands on her skin instead of the leaves of his bouquets.

'I bet I'm allergic to ivy,' Paula muttered direfully, pushing the stuff away.

She was certainly allergic to him. Ever since she had met him, he had lodged in some deep part of her mind like a needle. Whenever she thought of him, she winced. When she wasn't thinking of him, there was still that profoundly uneasy feeling of something painful waiting to stab at her again. Yet what was it he had done that was so painful?

He had been rude about Trish, true. Well, she had been rude right back. He had tried to pull her strings. But she had told him she wouldn't work for him on his trumped-up excuse. So she had won that one too. And as for his outrageous proposition—well, she had stamped on that at once.

Not, thought Paula ruefully, that Eduardo had seemed exactly crushed by her response. Rather the reverse, if anything, she thought. He'd looked amused, as if he relished the challenge. And didn't doubt the ultimate outcome.

That was annoying, of course, but it was hardly painful. So why this shivery feeling that Eduardo Mascherini might be lethal to her? Could he be right when he said there was something special between them?

'Ridiculous,' Paula said sharply, out loud.

Remember, even his cousin says he's a bastard to his women. And he doesn't care about anything but his company.

And even while he's been throwing sexual invitations at me he's had Gina Pesce in residence in that flat of his.

She threw the detective novel away from her.

Music, she thought. That was what she needed. Something loud and passionate that would knock all thoughts of anything else out of her head. Opera, that would do it. Tragic opera for preference.

The Unknown Prince was vowing that he would be victorious in the morning when the doorbell rang insistently. Paula jumped. She looked at her watch. Not far short of midnight. She knew who it was.

She stood up, smoothing her green velvet trousers with hands that shook a little. Then she squared her shoulders and went to answer him.

The bell ran again imperatively. When she opened the door Eduardo Mascherini was leaning on the doorbell. He was dressed in a dinner-jacket with a white silk scarf looped negligently round his neck. He was looking alert and amused and just a touch impatient.

Behind her the music arched and soared. His brows rose.

'Opera fan?'

'Sometimes,' said Paula uncommunicatively. She stood aside. 'You'd better come in.'

The look of amusement deepened. 'Gracious,' he murmured, stepping on to the polished parquet.

She shut the door behind him.

'Well, I wasn't expecting a visit. I asked you to phone me.'

He took off his scarf and dropped it on the wooden chest.

'I always find it more satisfactory to negotiate face to face,' he said smoothly.

Recalling what he had wanted to negotiate the last time they met, Paula raised her chin in defiance.

'I called you because Trish and Franco have been to see me,' she said hastily.

He wasn't a bit disconcerted. 'I thought they might.'

He took her by the elbow and led her back into the sitting-room.

The Ministers were now offering the Unknown Prince anything his heart desired if he'd only tell them his secret name. Or alternatively go away and stop upsetting everyone. Paula knew how they felt.

She switched off the amplifier with a quick movement. In the sudden silence her visitor surveyed her.

'You look tired,' he said abruptly.

Paula pushed a hand through her loosened hair, suddenly self-conscious. She avoided his eyes, though she knew he watched the movement.

'There's a lot going on,' she said ruefully. 'And it's too long since I had a holiday. Nothing I'm not used to.'

He leaned his shoulder against the door-jamb.

'I'd put in a bid for that holiday,' he said frankly. 'You've got shadows under your eyes a vampire would envy.'

Paula stiffened. She would have retorted in kind except that he looked full of vitality, in spite of the hour. And what he said about her own appearance was probably true, she knew.

So she shrugged the criticism away. 'It comes of being fair-skinned. It means nothing. You won't recognise me in the morning after a good night's sleep.'

His mouth slanted. 'Not sleeping too well?'

'No, I'm sleeping fine...'

'Neither am I,' he said as if she hadn't spoken.

Another curse of fair skin was that too easy colour, Paula thought. She was furious with herself and him as she felt her skin redden uncontrollably.

'That's nothing to do with me,' she said hastily.

He gave her another of those laughing sexy looks that made her feel as if she was balancing on a precipice.

'You are so wrong,' he murmured.

'Stop it.' Paula was almost shouting, she realised.

His brows rose. She bit her lip.

'Look, just stop it. I know you think this is funny, but my sense of humour isn't that good when my sister's life is on the line.'

He said drily, 'I don't think either of us is losing sleep because of your sister, Paula.'

'I—am—not—losing—sleep,' she hissed.

His mouth quirked. 'Fair enough. What am I doing here, then?'

'I told you. They've been to see me. They——' she drew a long breath '—they want to get married.'

There was a little silence. She had the feeling that his brain was working at lightning speed, though his face was perfectly expressionless.

Then he said again, 'I thought they might.' He sounded perfectly indifferent. It was oddly chilling.

'They want you to persuade Franco's mother to come to the wedding. He's told her and she's not best pleased, I gather.'

He shrugged. 'Predictable.'

'Well, will you?'

He looked at her thoughtfully. 'This was Franco's idea?'

'He seemed to think you'd be able to talk her into it,' she admitted frankly.

He looked bored. 'I probably could.' He laughed softly. 'And Franco knew I wouldn't get involved. So he set you to talk me into it. Am I right?' There was no point in denying it. 'Shrewd of him. Perhaps there's more to Franco than I suspected.'

Paula didn't want to enquire too closely into that oblique remark.

'Will you do it, then?'

There was a pause. 'Give me one good reason why I should,' he said at last.

'It would make Trish happy,' Paula said simply.

His mouth quirked. 'And it is so important that this little sister has everything she wants?'

Paula flushed and looked down. 'No, of course not. Only—you must understand—we never had much of a family life. Trish is very—loving. She wants to start off her married life in a reasonable relationship with Franco's family.'

'She's on to a loser there,' he said cynically. 'I've never found that family having reasonable relationships. Still less affectionate ones.'

Paula was shocked. It was, after all, his own family he was talking about. She bit her lip.

'Trish has always wanted to be part of a large family,' she said at last in a low voice. 'There were only two of us and she—well, you've met her.'

'Yes,' he said in an odd voice. 'Yes, I've met her. And I agree with you. A heart like warm butter. You've got all the steel in the family, haven't you, Paula?'

'I would never have believed you were sisters,' he had said.

Paula winced. It was crazy. She knew she was tough. She had set out to be tough. She was even proud of it. So why did this man, saying that she was made of steel, fill her with a sudden wild regret?

She said quietly, 'That's probably true.'

'And if you loved a man, you wouldn't care what his mother thought about it.'

'That would depend on the man and the mother,' she hedged.

'No, it wouldn't,' he said positively. 'If you were in love, you wouldn't care about the whole damned world.'

Paula looked away. Neil had cared. And she had gone along with it, the secrecy and the lies. It was only in retrospect she had realised how much she had hated it; how much it hurt. Eduardo was right. She wouldn't ever do that again.

She said carefully, 'Well, that's not likely to happen at my age. And it's got nothing to do with what Trish feels. She wants the family rejoicing when she gets married. And it looks as if she won't get it unless you intervene.'

'You mean Franco's mother is in a tantrum,' Eduardo interpreted. He was looking bored again. 'I dare say she is. She's never wanted to believe that Franco was grown up. Pushes her out of the younger generation.'

Paula was curious. 'Is that awkward? For you, I mean.'

'She won't force me to sack him, if that's what you mean,' he said, amused. 'She isn't that big a shareholder. And anyway they all know I don't take orders

from feuding family members. There was too much of
that in my grandfather's day.'

Paula was intrigued. But she didn't ask. She didn't
want him to think she was interested in him in any way.
She didn't want to admit it herself.

'But will you talk to her?'

'I might.' His expression was enigmatic.

Her eyes narrowed. 'On conditions?'

Eduardo smiled. It was a slow, confident smile and it
sent little shivers up and down her spine. 'Of course.'

'What?'

'You know, I like that air of innocence,' he said conversationally. 'The contrast with the businesswoman
image is very—intriguing.'

Somewhere in her breast her heart began to flutter.
Paula repressed alarm. I am an independent, adult
woman and I can handle this, she told herself.

She managed a rueful smile and shook her head. 'That
wasn't what you said the first time you——'

His eyes were dancing at the memory.

'The first time you let your hair down with me?' he
suggested.

Paula swallowed. At his words a disturbingly explicit
memory presented itself.

'The first time we met,' she corrected him. 'As I remember you told me not to play the innocent because
it didn't suit me.'

'I was wrong.'

Paula shivered at the low, caressing note.

'Don't forget I thought it was you who was having
the affair with him,' Eduardo reminded her. 'I didn't
believe in the innocence. And I don't like being manipu-
lated. I didn't know Trish existed. And of course I wanted
to protect him from you.'

It was oddly hurtful. She looked away.

'Well, you don't have to worry now...'

He put his hands on her shoulders and her voice drained abruptly into silence.

'I couldn't let him get entangled with a woman I was going to have to take off him, now could I?' Eduardo murmured outrageously.

Paula thought suddenly, It is after midnight, I am alone in the flat with this man and I don't think he has any scruples at all. This is not *safe*.

She removed herself from his light embrace.

'You'll talk to his mother? Then we can all dance at the wedding. I said I'd call them tomorrow.'

He eyed her with frustration.

'You don't give an inch, do you?'

Not with you, she thought. I can't afford to. Though she didn't quite know why.

'I don't think I understand you.'

'Of course you do.' He was impatient, though the humour still lurked in his eyes. 'You've been fighting mad with me ever since we met. To be honest I don't entirely blame you. But it's time to drop the hostilities, forget the irrelevancies and start dealing for ourselves.'

'Dealing?'

'The cards we've been given.'

'You think we're playing some sort of game?'

His smile was vivid, giving the dark, dramatic face a blinding charm. Paula blinked.

'Of course we are. Or we will as soon as you stop running away from me.'

'I don't play games,' said Paula decisively.

'No, I know. It shows. Never mind,' he said with odious sympathy, 'you'll soon get the hang of it. You've got a lot to learn but I'm an excellent teacher.'

She looked him up and down, grey eyes glinting.

'Modest, too.'

He gave another shout of laughter. 'False modesty's a waste of time. Like every other sort of lying. Like what you're doing now.' He didn't touch her but Paula tensed as if he were going to. 'Life's too short to pretend,' he said. 'You'll find out. For the sake of my sanity, I hope it's sooner rather than later.'

Paula could have danced with frustration. Whatever she said, he seemed to bring the conversation back to the same subject: the one subject she couldn't deal with.

'What are your conditions?' she said hardily. 'For speaking to Franco's mother, I mean,' she added hastily, seeing the glint in his eye.

'That you come with me,' he said.

Paula swallowed. 'You mean she's here? In London?'

'No.'

She hadn't really thought he did.

'I can't go to Italy. I've only just got back from New York. I'm up to my eyes in work.'

'How important is your sister?'

'What?'

'Those are my conditions,' he said. It was quite gentle. And quite implacable.

Paula shut her eyes for a moment, marshalling her arguments. 'That's nonsense. I'm not going to have any influence with Signora Gratz. You'd be better taking whatever-her-name-is. Gina somebody.'

The distinctive eyebrows flew up.

'So you know about Gina?'

'I'm told everyone does,' Paula whipped back before she thought.

Eduardo looked amused, the handsome mouth slanting. Paula bit her lip. She had sounded like a jealous woman, she thought, humiliated. He was too acute to miss that note of resentment. His whole expression said that he hadn't missed it.

She put a hand to her suddenly burning cheek.

'Not that it's anything to do with me,' she said swiftly, trying to retrieve the slip. 'But wouldn't what's-her-name be more able to persuade Franco's mother?'

'Her name is Gina Pesce,' Eduardo said gently.

'Signorina Pesce. She would surely be more appropriate than me.'

'But you see, I don't want Gina Pesce,' he said. 'I want you.'

Paula met his eyes, half excited, half ashamed. They both knew he wasn't talking about a family negotiation. Paula felt a wave of dizziness sweep over her.

He's a bastard to his women, she reminded herself. Wasn't he demonstrating it even now? He was certainly not showing much consideration for Gina Pesce. And, for all Paula knew, the woman was upstairs in his flat waiting for him to go back to her.

How could she respond to him like this? Her heart fluttered crazily. And she didn't even trust him.

She said with an effort, 'As I'm not available, that's not relevant, I'm afraid.'

His eyes narrowed.

'What would make you available?'

She moistened her lips. 'Nothing.' Her voice was not much more than a croak, Paula thought in disgust.

To her astonishment he swore softly and virulently. She didn't understand the words but the meaning was plain enough.

Quite suddenly he reached for her. Paula was not expecting it or she would have had time to take evasive action. Or that was what she told herself afterwards.

His mouth was hard, without kindness or affection. This was quite simply a man who was used to taking what he wanted without too much trouble, suddenly finding that this one wasn't going to be easy. The anger was almost tangible.

Paula's head fell back. She moaned. She pressed her hands against his chest, trying to push him away, but she felt as if all her muscles had turned to water. Against the hard wall of his chest she hadn't the strength of a mouse. He certainly didn't appear to notice her resistance.

Eventually he raised his head. The eyes that burned down into hers were the grey of thunderclouds, almost black and burning with an emotion that was all too evident.

It was not, Paula noted, love.

She hauled herself away. She was trembling so badly that she felt as if she could barely stand upright. Unobtrusively, she put a hand behind her and steadied herself against the wooden chest.

'Then by God I shall make you available,' he swore.

And before she could answer he was banging the door behind him.

CHAPTER SEVEN

THE flowers died in time. The memory of that last encounter did not fade so readily. Especially as Paula soon found out what he meant by his final threat.

For a couple of days there was silence. She worked like mad. Trish rang her once to find out the result of her interview with Eduardo. Paula said that she had better talk to him herself and, pleading work, rang off.

Sarah, who was with her when the call came through, raised her eyebrows.

'I thought we weren't working for the Dreamboat?'

'We aren't.'

'But you just said...'

'That was a personal call,' Paula said with dignity.

If possible Sarah's eyebrows climbed higher. But she said nothing more. Or not until she came in with a file three days later.

'Project Fortification,' she said, putting it down in front of Paula. 'Someone thinks you're working for him. Even if you don't.'

Paula's stomach felt as if she were in a lift that had suddenly lost its cables.

'That was a joke,' she said uncertainly.

Sarah patted the bulging file. 'A nice fat fee-earning joke,' she said drily. 'Marriott would like to be kept informed.'

She went out.

With a sinking heart, Paula pulled the file towards her. She had been so certain that there was no take-over;

that he had been talking entirely about herself and her sister; that he was amusing himself at her expense.

She turned over the pages. She was wrong. There was a real acquisition here. Though it was one that only a real pirate would go after, she thought. Reluctant admiration stirred at his daring.

She rang his office. He took her call at once.

'You realise it's a crazy idea?' she said without preamble.

He chuckled. 'The merchant bankers wouldn't be pleased to hear you say that. They think it's perfectly feasible.'

'They're thinking of their fees,' she said crisply. 'It'll cost you a fortune. And if the management leave it won't be worth a tenth of what you'll have to pay for it.'

'So draw me up an acquisition document that ties the management into the deal for five years,' he said at once.

She sighed. 'Have you any idea how difficult it is to make something like that stick?'

'I thrive on difficulties,' he said. 'And so do you.'

Paula drew a long breath. 'Well, actually I'm very busy,' she began. 'It would really be much better if someone else handles this one. Kit or——'

'Paula?'

'Yes?'

'You or no one,' he said softly. 'I've already told Marriott.'

'That's not fair.'

'I'm not fair,' he said unanswerably.

'But——'

'Try and give it to anyone else and I take all the Isola business somewhere else. There are plenty of good lawyers in London. The merchant bank are itching to recommend one.'

'This is so unprofessional,' she began.

Eduardo laughed. 'You or no one,' he repeated.

He rang off without giving her time to reply.

She tried to persuade Kit Marriott to give the work to someone else, of course. But whatever Eduardo had said to him had made him adamant.

She returned chastened from her interview with the senior partner to the unwelcome news that the Conte was waiting to see her.

Paula knew when she was beaten. She went to the waiting area.

He was standing by a tall parlour palm, looking out into the street. His hands were in the pockets of his exquisitely cut jacket and he was half turned away from her. He looked serious and preoccupied.

It startled Paula a little. She had grown used to seeing him in quite another guise, teasing, negligently assured, with that deadly laughter in his eyes. This withdrawn man was a stranger.

But as soon as he saw her he was himself again. He came towards her, both hands spread flat.

'The beautiful Miss Castle,' he said caressingly, to Paula's annoyance and the receptionist's avid delight.

He took the hand she was holding out to him and kissed it. It was no courteous brush of the lips across the air above her knuckles but a real kiss. Devoutly hoping she didn't look as embarrassed as she felt, Paula retrieved her hand.

'How nice to see you. Though you needn't have troubled to come to the office, Count Mascherini,' she said coolly.

He quirked an eyebrow. 'You would have come to mine?'

Conscious of listening ears, Paula said repressively, 'When necessary, of course.'

He chuckled. 'You're a liar.'

'Please come into an interview-room,' Paula said with a smile that should have wiped the smile off his face.

Not noticeably repentant, he followed her.

'Now look,' she said, the moment the door closed, 'you may be able to make me work for you but that doesn't mean you can embarrass me in front of the staff. We've got to have some rules here.'

'Your rules?' he asked, eyebrows raised. 'Or mine?'

'Mine,' said Paula firmly.

He shook his head. 'I play by my own rules.'

A bastard to his women, Paula remembered. Well, she wasn't one of his women yet. And if she kept her head and an armour of professional conduct firmly in place, please, God, she never would be. No matter what the devilish Count intended. Or, for that matter, what her own treacherous feelings might prompt.

She said slowly, 'What gives you the right to behave like this? Do you think you're entitled to because you pay the bills?'

'When I pay the piper I call the tune,' he agreed.

Paula flushed. 'You only pay this piper in the office. Is that clear?'

'There is much more between you and me than a small business project,' he said softly.

Paula drew herself to her full height.

'No, there isn't.'

'Oh, yes. From the first time.'

She closed her eyes to break the mesmeric contact with his.

'Are you always like this?' she said in despair.

'In matters of love and business I find it generally pays to come straight to the point,' he said coolly.

Her eyes flew open, startled. *Love*?

He gave a soft laugh. 'So there shall be no misunderstandings.'

No, not love. Or not as she understood it anyway.

'Oh, I don't think there are any misunderstandings,' Paula said a trifle grimly. 'You think it would be amusing to have a brief fling with a lady lawyer who doesn't want you. Probably because she doesn't want you.'

He looked reproachful. 'Who said anything about brief? Besides, you do want me.'

That was all too close to the truth, as Paula was honest enough to admit to herself.

'You don't have much respect for women, do you?' she said.

An expression of distaste crossed his face. 'As much as they deserve.'

She said wearily. 'And have I deserved to be hounded like this?'

That disconcerted him. She saw it at once.

He said slowly, 'Most women would find it flattering, I think—to have a man pursue them because he cannot help himself.'

Paula shook her head. 'Not me. I think you must have known the wrong women.'

The handsome mouth was suddenly cynical.

'That is all too possible.'

She thought of Gina Pesce who was glamorous enough to intimidate Trish.

'So what do you want with me?' she cried in despair.

His look was full of irony.

'All right, all right. I know what you *want*,' she admitted. 'But *why*?'

His eyes were light and brilliant as sunlight glancing off a rapier.

'There is something special there. Don't ask me why.' He shrugged. 'You feel it too. If you were more experienced you would recognise it.'

Paula stared at him. She saw he was serious.

'What about Gina Pesce?' she said in a harsh voice.

A graceful gesture dismissed Gina Pesce. It was chilling.

'So she doesn't count any more?' Paula asked sweetly. 'Now that you've seen a different toy and you want that?'

Eduardo frowned. 'I don't regard you or any woman as a toy.'

'What, then?'

The look he flashed her was a challenge.

'An intelligent adult. One who knows what she wants and takes it.'

'No matter what the price?' Paula muttered under her breath.

His eyes narrowed. 'I think you must have known the wrong men if you talk about love like that,' he told her softly.

'Oh, I have,' Paula agreed fervently. She met his eyes limpidly. 'Men who use words like love very lightly. And the meaning changes with circumstances.'

There was a little silence. They stared at each other like duellists.

Then he said abruptly, 'Have dinner with me. Not because I've threatened Kit Marriott, because you—because we have unfinished business. And this isn't the place to discuss it.'

'We're in agreement on that, at least,' Paula said drily.

'Will you come?'

She looked at the dark face and saw it was implacable. She already felt as if she'd been through a twenty-four-hour negotiation. If she was going to get any work done in the rest of the day, she had to persuade him to go and leave her in peace. She sighed, dipping her head in acquiescence.

'Tonight,' he said. 'The penthouse.'

'Very well.'

He looked at her across the room. She felt as if a strong magnet was drawing her. Her head went back with the force of resisting it.

Eduardo said softly, 'If you don't arrive I shall come and fetch you. From wherever you are.'

Paula's mouth quirked wryly.

'I believe you. I'll be there.'

He laughed suddenly. 'I think you will. And now...'

At once Paula was tense. But he was tossing a slim document on the table.

'The bank's projections. I thought you should have them,' he said blandly. 'Before you advise me on how to tie these people to me indissolubly, you'd better see who is critical.'

Paula picked it up and held it against her chest like a shield. 'Thank you,' she said with restraint.

She showed him out. His farewell was marginally less flamboyant than his greeting but the damage was done. In a glance under her lashes at the palpitating receptionist, Paula saw that she had become the heroine of the latest office romance.

'Damn,' she said under her breath and retired to the ladies' room to restore her equilibrium.

The face in the mirror looked the same. Eyes a little wider, perhaps. Mouth a little more vulnerable. But basically still Paula Castle, career woman and mistress of her destiny. And yet... And yet... She looked as if something had changed her. As if she'd touched some magic talisman.

She sat down slowly on one of the small gilt chairs. She shook her head as if to clear it. Was he right, then? Was there something special between them? And special in what way?

He'd made it plain that he wanted her all right. He found her attractive and so he wanted what he was used to: a temporary affair. It would be casual, companionable; probably amusing; certainly passionate. And presumably the tacit understanding was that it stayed uncommitted on both sides.

Paula knew instinctively that that wouldn't do for her. Not that she wanted to commit herself to him. Of course she didn't. But if nothing else Neil had taught her that you needed to know what you were doing before you embarked on one of these elegant semi-detached affairs. She hadn't done ten years ago.

She contemplated the skills and emotional resilience it would take to deal with Eduardo Mascherini now.

'Oh, hell,' she said slowly.

It wasn't only that she wasn't young and innocent any more. There was more to it than that. She was thirty-one. If she started a relationship now it would be serious.

Paula thought about having a serious relationship with the laughing sophisticate she had just said goodbye to. Her heart began to flutter again in a way that was becoming disturbingly familiar.

What is happening to me? she thought. Am I afraid of the man? If I am, *why*? And if not, why can't I get him out of my mind?

All too vividly, Eduardo Mascherini's sardonic features came into her mind. She closed her eyes.

'He is nothing to do with me,' she said out loud. It didn't sound very convincing. 'Oh, this is crazy. He said *love*. But he doesn't love me. I don't even want him to.'

In fact Paula gave a small shudder at the thought. She could imagine few things more frightening than being the object of Eduardo Mascherini's affection. The edgy attention he bestowed on her, somewhere between amusement and lust, was more than she could handle as it was. If he really *cared* . . . She curbed her wayward thoughts.

'Be yourself,' she advised her mirrored image curtly.
'He's used to glamour. And he's used to ladies who play
by his rules. Make sure he knows where you stand and
he'll leave you alone.'

It was still an act of will to leave the quiet haven of
the ladies' room and go back to work. She was absent-
minded throughout the rest of the day. To such an extent,
indeed, that she had to stay later than she'd intended in
order to finish the work she had set herself.

When the phone rang the secretaries had gone and the
city night outside the window was a profound black,
studded with the street-signs and the arc lights picking
out the architectural features of a nearby Wren church.

Paula was bent over a complicated problem, books
open all around her, her desk illuminated only by a pool
of light from the angled lamp. At the shrill sound, she
jumped, knocking one of the books to the floor.

It was an apologetic night porter.

'Sorry to disturb you, Miss Castle. Conte Mascherini
on the line. Thought you'd want to speak to him.'

Paula winced. There was no reason for it. The man
had said nothing at which she could take offence. But
she sensed that he had heard the gossip and thought this
was Eduardo setting up a romantic assignation somewhere. The thought that it would amuse Eduardo immensely did nothing to reconcile her to being the subject
of such speculation.

Paula sighed, easing herself upright. She had a burning
pain between the shoulderblades and her eyes were
blurring. Too much tension, she knew. Too much work,
too much tension, not enough exercise, not enough rest.

'Put the call through,' she said wearily.

She put a hand on the back of her neck and stretched,
circling her head. This tiredness was getting beyond a
joke, she thought, hearing her joints crack. She must

get Sarah to book her into a health farm for a few days. She made a note on the pad in front of her.

There was a hint of laughter in the smooth voice when he was put through.

'Am I coming to get you?'

She looked at her watch, startled. 'I didn't realise how late it is. No, you needn't bother. I'll come quietly.'

'I've never had one of my dinner invitations sound like a prison sentence before,' he said. He sounded amused, she thought but something else as well. Was it angry?

'Sorry about that.' She didn't mean it and it didn't sound as if she did.

'No, you aren't,' he corrected. 'But I will pretend you are. And you will certainly be sorry if you don't arrive. Shall we say—in an hour?'

Paula agreed numbly. Oh, well, better get it out of the way, she thought, stacking the books with their myriad place markers. It wouldn't do her any good at all to have to sweat through another day with the prospect of an interview with Mascherini to look forward to at the end of it. He didn't sound as if he would be graceful about a lady standing him up, even with the best of excuses.

She picked up a cab almost at once. In the flat she changed into a black cocktail dress with a dramatic silver peacock on the right shoulder. It was part of her uniform of the successful professional woman. She could not remember ever having worn it to a private engagement before. But it was armour and tonight, Paula thought wryly, she could do with all the armour she could get.

She had expected him to answer the door to her himself, his mouth quirking in that hateful amusement. But her ring was greeted by a beautifully attired manservant.

He ushered her in, took her coat, led her to where the Conte was sitting among his collection of art and gave her a drink as Mascherini rose gracefully to greet her. Paula shook hands, ignoring the glint in the Conte's eyes. As she had expected: amusement.

She braced herself. But Eduardo was a model of the courteous host. Puccini, muted and seductive, poured out of the sound system. They dined alone. But he barely touched her, other than to pull out her chair for her or to retrieve the heavy linen napkin that slid from her knees more than once. And the manservant was hardly out of her sight for the rest of the evening. It was too good to last, of course.

Eventually there was some small sign from her host; so small that she did not see it, only the man's reaction. She tensed at once. It was too late.

With a little nod the manservant left. There was something final about the gentle but decisive gesture with which he pulled the double doors shut after him. It couldn't have been more obvious that they were alone in the suite and would be left so until the morning. Paula felt her nerves tauten a fraction.

Eduardo said easily, 'I won't ask you to breach your principles by pouring the coffee.'

She said, 'No coffee for me, thank you.'

His eyebrows lifted. 'I hadn't taken you for an anti-caffeine activist as well.' There was an edge to his voice.

Paula didn't ask as well as what.

She said hastily, 'I'm just not very fond of coffee. Especially at night. It seems to keep me awake...'

She heard her voice trail off as that edged smile of his appeared. He said deliberately, 'Tonight I would certainly prefer that it was not Bernardino's excellent coffee that was responsible for your wakefulness.'

Paula worked that one out. Though she did not really need to. He had already told her, with every word and glance, what it was that he expected of the evening. And soon enough he would touch.

She had ignored it all evening. But it was there, just below the civilised surface. Paula had tried hard to feel reassured by the impersonal conversation, by the re-straining presence of Bernardino. But all the time she had seen the quiet triumph in those cold eyes and known that the civilised conversation was a gigantic bluff.

Suddenly she realised that she had been deceiving herself when she refused to recognise it. Worse, she had been allowing him to pretend that her presence here was tacit acceptance. But it wasn't. The triumph was tem-porary. No man was ever going to celebrate victory in the morning over Paula Castle.

And now she was going to have to tell him so. She swallowed.

He poured himself coffee. The cup was exquisite, a simple landscape brush-painted on to the eggshell-thin porcelain in a few simple strokes. Paula concentrated hard on the quality of the workmanship. It was easier than meeting his eyes.

She said carefully, 'I must be going soon. I have a lot of work to catch up on. I promised my assistant an early start tomorrow.'

She didn't know what she expected. A protest perhaps? Maybe even some explosion of anger. Mascherini was a powerful man. He might choose to think himself insulted.

But he said nothing. She could feel him watching her. It was an act of will to keep her eyes fixed on the cup in his hands. She could feel the determination in him that she should look up and meet his eyes.

At last he moved. Paula tensed at once. But all he was doing was settling back in the elegant chair, crossing one exquisitely tailored leg over the other.

Then he said very softly, 'I think not.'

Her eyes flew to his then. There would, she thought with some distant remnants of self-mockery, be no mistaking their expression. Stark alarm.

Eduardo's brows twitched together in a frown. Paula fought down the panic, her eyes falling.

'I assure you I am very busy,' she said with a fair assumption of calm. But she didn't risk looking at him again.

'I am sure you are.' He sounded amused.

The pause that followed was deliberate, she was sure. It put her on the defensive. She swallowed.

'Then you'll understand...'

'No,' he said quietly.

Paula looked at the clock. It was eleven. Surely not too soon for a polite guest to be making a move to the door?

She said coolly, 'Clients expect a prompt reply, you know. You will understand that, at least. And I have many clients apart from yourself. You should have some fellow feeling. I can't neglect them for you.'

Eduardo said with precision, 'Just at this moment I do not look on myself as one of your clients.'

Paula flushed. 'No. Of course not. I didn't mean...'

'Didn't you?' His voice was meditative. 'And yet I have the distinct impression that you are telling me— very gently, very politely—that you have been having this dinner with me entirely under protest because I am a client of your firm.'

She shifted uncomfortably. 'I appreciate this opportunity to—er—iron out past misunderstandings, of course——'

'No,' he said again, interrupting her.

His voice was like velvet. He still hadn't moved. There was no reason for her heart to clench in that explicit, all too familiar chill. She moistened her lips.

'There was no misunderstanding,' Eduardo said levelly. 'I have wanted you from the first time we met. We have both known it. Though we may not have liked it.' He laughed soundlessly. 'I cannot remember when I have been angrier. But it was still there, wasn't it?'

Paula didn't answer. Her heart was thundering somewhere up in her throat. Perhaps I shall faint, she thought hopefully. But she didn't.

After a pause he said, 'It is still there for both of us. What you choose to do about it is, of course, up to you.'

Paula still said nothing.

His voice sharpened. 'But don't pretend you don't know what I'm talking about.'

She weighed her words carefully. 'I'm not sure that I do. That first time, you were very angry, of course. So was I at the time. In retrospect it is understandable, of course. I agree that things got a little out of hand.'

'You were more than angry.' His voice was like a stone thrown into a crowd, silencing her. 'And so was I.' He put his coffee-cup down.

Paula said hastily, 'I was very tired. Jet-lagged. I'd just come back from the States.'

He stood up.

Her voice rose. 'I'd got straight on to a plane after an all-night meeting. I was worried about Trish . . .'

He pulled her sharply to her feet and kissed her. She was awkward in his arms, like a scarecrow. Her limbs felt clumsy, as if they didn't belong to her. She breathed the smell of coffee; then that subtle aftershave that smelled like cool interiors on a hot afternoon. His, of course. She should have known it. She shut her mind and her senses to the gentle brush of his mouth across hers.

When he let her go, there was absolute silence.

He said under his breath, 'Why are you doing this? Pretending there's nothing there? You must know...'

His eyes searched her face. She thought suddenly, He thinks I'm a sophisticated woman. And I'm not. He thinks I can handle a temporary affair. And I can't. When he left me I'd be devastated.

The realisation hit her like an electric shock. Paula jerked once in his arms and was still. Then, drawing a deep breath, she stepped away from him. It was a neat movement. The clumsiness, the internal devastation wasn't showing yet.

'There is nothing there,' she said steadily. She crossed her fingers behind her back in pure reflex. She was hoping against hope that it was true.

She twitched her shoulders. His hands fell away.

'I'm beginning to think you don't know what you're talking about.' Astonishingly, he sounded amused again.

'I assure you I do.'

And she did, Paula thought sadly. More than he or anyone else could guess at.

She looked at her watch ostentatiously. 'I should go. It's later than I thought.'

Eduardo gave a soft laugh. 'Too late.'

She shot him a startled look. He returned it calmly. He made no move to touch her again. She withdrew a couple of unobtrusive steps.

'You're not intending to keep me here by force, I hope?' She managed to sound amused but all her defences were alert.

'Not unless you insist,' he agreed.

He was smiling. She stared at him, confused. He sounded almost indulgent, Paula thought suddenly. As if she were very young. As if he was humouring her. Her pride revolted at his tone.

'I insist,' she said crisply, 'on going home when I choose. Now. Perhaps I could have my coat?'

He shook his head, laughing a little. He made no move to collect her coat from the hall cupboard. Instead he seated himself on the deep sofa and relaxed into its cushions, one arm along the back. He smiled up at her. She might just as well not have spoken, Paula thought, her temper beginning to rise.

'Punishing me for my unworthy suspicions, my dear? But I've admitted I was wrong. I've made amends. After all, Trish has more grounds than you to be angry with me. And she has been very forgiving.'

'Trish,' said her fond sister between her teeth, 'is a fool.'

The dark eyebrows flew up.

'That's rather harsh. I thought she was charming.'

Paula caught herself. 'I'm glad,' she said colourlessly. 'It's just as well since you're going to be related.'

The cool eyes gleamed. 'It is indeed,' he agreed courteously. 'And in the circumstances makes her the reverse of a fool, wouldn't you say?' He paused and tilted his head up to her, his mouth slanting in the wicked grin she was coming to know. 'So where does that leave you?'

She looked down at him, confused. 'Me?'

He laughed softly. 'You, my—cousin-in-law-to-be. My prickly, hostile, dishonest cousin-in-law-to-be.'

That stung. 'Dishonest?' she flashed.

Eduardo Mascherini stayed calm. 'Dishonest,' he repeated in amusing tone. 'Now why?'

Paula gave an impatient exclamation. 'Oh, you're ridiculous!' she said. 'I'll get my own coat.'

She went to the door. But she made the mistake of glancing back at the handsome face, and made an unwelcome discovery. The grey eyes were not amused at all. Nor cool now.

'Paula,' he said softly.

She stopped dead, as if he'd thrown magician's dust over her.

This is ridiculous, she thought frantically. I'm an independent woman. He has no power over me. I can walk out if I want. I *can*.

But her limbs felt unnaturally light. They trembled as if she had no power of movement left until her opponent chose to let her go.

'What are you afraid of?' he asked gently.

She set her jaw. 'I am not,' said Paula tightly, 'afraid of anything.'

She would have given anything for it to be true.

'Then come and sit here and tell me why you're still angry with me.'

'I am not angry with you,' she very nearly shouted.

He laughed aloud at that. 'It doesn't sound like it.' He stopped lounging suddenly and sat up. 'I am not a schoolboy, Paula. I have had my share of lovers. And I've seen relationships tear other people apart. Is that what you're afraid of?' His voice softened. 'It wouldn't. I would take care of you, I promise.' He touched the cushioned seat. 'Come here. You don't need to be afraid of me.'

Paula found it would be all too easy to obey that casual command. She sat herself rather hastily on the arm of the nearest chair and clutched her hands together to hide their trembling.

'Your rules,' she said in a carefully neutral voice. 'That's what you said. It doesn't sound like a good risk to me. How do the lovers feel when you move on? You may not be torn apart but what about them? The Gina Pesces of this world.'

His brows twitched together. 'You don't even know Gina.'

'I know about her,' Paula said quietly.

'You listen to gossip?' He was scornful.

Her mouth twisted. 'It's not exactly gossip when you might follow in someone's footsteps.'

Eduardo said with sudden harshness, 'Gina Pesce is a cold and calculating woman who thinks she would like to join the Isola family. She and my half-sister have been plotting to get me married to her for the most of the last fifteen years. I have never given her reason. I have certainly never taken her to bed. There are no footsteps to follow.' His eyes were like stone. 'Does that answer the gossips?' he said contemptuously.

Paula was taken aback. 'But she was staying with you.'

'Franco,' he detected suddenly. He was impatient. 'She was staying in the apartment. It belongs to the company. There are eight bedrooms here. I have no idea which one Bernardino gave Gina. She was here for some damned fashion show. Or that's what she said. She was here when I flew in. I was not aware that she was. As soon as the fashion show was over she left. At my request.'

Paula was chastened. 'I'm—sorry.'

'What do you think I am, for God's sake?' he said. 'Did you think I was pursuing you while I kept my resident mistress at home?'

She whitened.

'You did.' He looked at her curiously. The anger seemed to seep out of him. He looked intrigued and faintly triumphant. 'You don't have much respect for men, do you, Paula?' he taunted softly.

She remembered her remark that afternoon and flushed. But she was not going to back down entirely.

'There have been other women,' she pointed out. 'You said so yourself.'

'I did, yes.' He looked surprised. 'What did you expect? I am not a child.'

Franco had said he was a bastard to his women. And Franco liked and respected him.

'Have they all gone quietly when you've finished with them?' she asked bitterly. 'Is that why you say you won't hurt me? Do you *notice* when you hurt people? Do you care what happens to them? After all, it was you who said we were playing a game. And that's what it is to you. A game.' She was almost in tears. 'A clever, cruel game. You don't really care one way or the other whether you get me into bed. Or any woman. You don't care what it costs us. All you care is that you win your damned *game.*'

He was very still suddenly; still and watchful. He said nothing. Paula became conscious that to a man of his perception she had probably said altogether too much.

She adopted a formal tone to cover the thickness in her throat, saying hurriedly, 'I am grateful for dinner and glad that we have cleared up our differences. All I want now——' for a nasty moment she thought her voice was going to break and the rest of the sentence came out rather crisper and faster than she intended '—is to go home to bed.'

There was a silence. She gave him a candid look, focusing carefully on a point a little to the left of his left eye.

'Thank you for a very pleasant evening. But now it's late and I must go.'

Eduardo said with the first hint of irritation he had shown, 'In a minute you'll tell me you don't mix business and pleasure.'

Paula could not control her slight, instinctive shudder. He frowned.

'Paula, what *is* it?' He stood up and came over to her, looking down at her intently. 'You're not a child. You know as well as I what there is between us. What there could be. All right, we started off badly and that was mostly my fault. But that is over. Now we have to go forward.'

She stood up. The movement was clumsy and she turned her ankle on the high, slim heel of her shoe. She put out a hand to the chair-back to steady herself. So it was starting to show now, she thought grimly. The panic. The helplessness.

She said harshly, '*We* don't have to do anything. You're making a mistake. There is nothing between us.'

He didn't touch her. He looked faintly puzzled.

'Nothing,' she repeated on a shout.

He was shaken by a soft laugh. 'Then why do you go up in flames when I touch you?'

Paula choked. 'I don't.'

'Oh, but you do. Even when you have the laser shields up as you have tonight.'

'I don't know what you're talking about,' she cried.

He reached out in an unexpected movement and seized her hand. Paula pulled away instinctively. But he didn't try to draw her into his arms again. He held her at arm's length and turned the pale wrist upwards. He feathered his thumb across it and she felt her pulse jump as if she had touched bare wires.

'When you're trying not to kiss me. This gives you away,' he said evenly.

Paula gave a small cry and snatched her hand away.

'You're impossible. It's ridiculous. I didn't have to *try* not to kiss you. I've never met a man I wanted to kiss less in my life,' she hurled at him.

His face was suddenly grim. 'Now that I believe,' he said unexpectedly. 'And what I want to know is—why?'

She hugged her wrist as if it had been burned.

'Is it so incredible that a woman might not want to kiss you?' she taunted, shaking.

He looked at her for a long moment. 'No. Of course not. But with an attraction like this...'

'There is no attraction.' Paula was almost weeping.

He shook his head. 'Then why are you still here, arguing with me? Why don't you just collect your coat and go?' he said softly. 'I'm not barring the door. I haven't slapped handcuffs on you. You don't even have to find a cab. All you do is walk out of the door and down the stairs and you're safe back in your fortress.'

Paula stared at him. It was true. She was deeply shaken. There was nothing keeping her here bandying words with him except her own desire for—what? A graceful farewell? A civilised pretence that there had been no hidden agenda of desire and acquisition here this evening?

But it was too late for that. She, at least, had gone beyond civilised pretences. Her uncertainty, her unreasoning panic were here in the room with them. He would have to be blind and deaf not to sense it. And Eduardo Mascherini was proving all too thoroughly that his senses were as alert as his intelligence. So why was she still here?

She said in a voice she didn't recognise, 'I hate you.' She took three wavering steps to the door.

He was there before her. This time he was barring the door. He leaned back against it, laughing a little. She stopped. He reached out and brought her body hard against his own.

'You should have taken your chance while you had it,' he said. He was amused, damn him. He was laughing at her.

Paula struggled to be angry. Anger was healing. Anger was strengthening. If she could be angry with him she might still get out of this luxurious trap with its Japanese porcelain and its seductive lighting with some dignity still intact. If she could be angry she might be able to ignore the remembered wretchedness that was sweeping through her, turning her muscles to ice and her mind to a jumble of half-formed pleas for mercy.

I won't beg, she thought. I won't.

He was running his hands down her spine as if she were a thing, she thought. As if she belonged to him and he could stroke her and bend her and play with her however he liked.

This was what Neil had done. This was where she had surrendered everything that she was, she reminded herself; and he had enjoyed it for a while until his real life had called him away. The old terrible feelings came back in a flood. There was a bitter taste in her mouth.

Eduardo kissed her neck, pushing the dark cloth away to touch his lips to the vulnerable skin below her collarbone. Paula's throat closed. Her eyes unfocused. She lost the sense of the room and the warmth and stillness. She even lost the sense of who it was who was touching her in this proprietorial way. She was back in the icy past.

'Trust me,' he was murmuring against her skin. 'Don't be afraid. I'd never hurt you. You know that.'

The irony of that penetrated her terrified mind as nothing else could have done. She began to laugh hysterically.

'Stop it.' He lifted his head abruptly. He gave her a slight shake. 'Stop it, Paula.'

She was trembling so hard that she could barely stand.

'How do you know what hurts me?' she said in a fierce whisper. 'How do you dare to think you know?'

He searched her face, his own alarmingly grim all of a sudden.

'This is not because of your sister,' he said. It wasn't a question. 'Or my imaginary mistresses.'

Paula put the back of her hand to her trembling mouth. His hands tightened on her shoulders.

'Let me go,' she said, her voice cracking.

He hesitated.

'Let me *go*.'

His hands fell away at once. Without their support, Paula swayed. Eduardo made a move as if to steady her and curbed it abruptly. He said, 'You'd better sit down.'

'I am going,' Paula said. Her voice was ragged.

She was beyond good manners, beyond dignity, beyond pretending that she had any sort of control left. She would never be able to face him again. She would certainly never be able to work for him. Maybe she would have to leave the firm. Her head was spinning.

'I am going. And you can't stop me,' she said in despair at the disaster she had made for herself.

He moved away from the door. 'No, I can't stop you,' he said quietly.

'I should never have come.' Paula said it more to herself than to him.

His eyes narrowed. She felt his eyes on her as she looked for her bag. She did her best to ignore it, trying with all her might to regain some sort of composure.

The bag was on the small lacquer table. She picked it up. Her hands, she saw, were still shaking very slightly but convulsively, as if she were very cold. She felt him notice that too and flushed.

It felt as if she had no modesty left, no secret he had not stripped and revealed to himself. And Eduardo Mascherini was not a man before whom she would have chosen to be naked, Paula thought. She put a hand on the doorknob as if it were the gate out of hell.

She did not look at him. She muttered some conventional farewell that he ignored.

'Will you answer me one question?' It was quiet, cool; no hint of recrimination or anger.

Paula hesitated.

'A very harmless question.'

She swallowed. 'All right.'

'The man you loved. The one you didn't live with,' he was choosing his words with care, 'do you still feel you need to be faithful?'

She looked at him then. His face was inscrutable.

'I don't understand.'

'No? Then let me be blunt. I find it difficult to believe that a woman of your intelligence should fail to realise that there was—or could be—something exceptional between you and me. So you must be blotting it out deliberately. I ask myself why.' He paused. 'It occurs to me that you might feel you are being disloyal to some memory.' He searched her face. 'Is that it, Paula? Should I have asked you about previous lovers?'

Paula looked down at her shaking hands. 'Lovers?' she said with bitterness. 'There was only one. And precious little love involved.'

Eduardo made a sharp little movement, then was still.

'I find that difficult to believe,' he said at last, very quietly. 'You——' He bit it off.

Oh, God, this was terrible. He wanted every last scrap of her self-respect. She wanted to scream, to rage and cry until she plunged into oblivion.

She squared her shoulders. This was melodrama, she told herself firmly. She was not going to cry in front of this man. That much at least she owed herself.

'Oh, I was in love,' she said at last, proudly. 'Too in love to see the signs.'

She thought there was a flash of something like admiration in his eyes. Which was, of course, ridiculous after the exhibition she had just made of herself.

'Will you tell me what happened?'

It was very gentle. The gentleness was nearly her undoing. She blinked rapidly, shaking her head. She thought he sighed.

'God damn it, why won't you tell me?' he said in an explosion of anger.

She flinched. At once his tone gentled again.

'I'm sorry. I never meant to distress you. It was—never mind. You are right, it's late and you should go home. I will see you to your door.' She flinched again and he added with sudden impatience, 'I've apologised, damn it. I won't lay a hand on you again. Stop looking at me like that.' Then, more gently, 'My dear, stop shaking. You have nothing to fear from me.'

And maybe that was true, Paula thought. Everything she'd feared—and more—seemed to have happened already. He had seen that she had no more poise than a neurotic schoolgirl, no more composure than a cornered wildcat. Any illusion he might have retained that she was the cool professional she wanted the world to think her was long gone. She bit her lip.

His mouth twisted. 'Come,' he said. 'You are tired. It will look better in the morning.'

She flashed him a startled glance. Was he a mind-reader?

He gave her a bleak smile. 'I am not entirely a fool.'

He opened the door for her. Bernardino was nowhere in sight. Presumably, thought Paula, wincing as the unpalatable idea presented itself, he would not have expected to see her off the premises. No doubt the Count would have made it plain that he expected his guest to stay the night.

'Is the breakfast tray for two already set in the kitchen?' she asked bitterly.

Eduardo stiffened. But he said levelly, 'I do not encourage Bernardino to interest himself in my private affairs—if that is what you're worried about.'

He held out her coat to her. She took it, careful not to touch him, and bundled it over her arm.

'I am not worried,' she said. 'And I am not your private affair.'

He made her a small mocking bow. 'As you have made patently clear this evening.'

She refused to blush. 'I'm glad we understand each other at last.'

He patted his inside pocket, assured himself that his lock card was in place and opened the front door for her. The carpeted hallway was eerily quiet.

Paula found herself whispering when she turned to say, 'There's no need to come down with me. I'm perfectly all right.'

'That I doubt. And I shall certainly come down. The least I can do,' he said drily, 'is see my date home.'

She shrugged and made for the stairs before he could call the lift. She could not face the enforced proximity. He made no comment. But when they stopped outside her door she saw in his face that he had seen through her stratagem. He didn't look offended, though; he looked intrigued. And the last thing she wanted was to intrigue Eduardo Mascherini.

She opened her door and turned. She didn't offer him her hand.

'Safe home. So this is goodbye,' she said. 'Thank you for the meal.'

She knew she had to say more than that to draw a line under the disastrous evening. She squared her shoulders and said with what dignity she could command, 'I am sorry that we misunderstood each other so drastically.'

'The meal,' he said courteously, 'was a pleasure. And you don't believe there was any misunderstanding. You think you understand me very well, I think. And I——'

Paula didn't see him move. But she was suddenly engulfed.

The kiss was long and passionately invasive. There was no pretending now that Eduardo wanted her for amusement only. Or that he didn't much care one way or the other whether he got her into bed in the end. Paula had never even imagined being kissed like that.

Shaken, she stared up at him, bruised lips parted. He touched her mouth very gently, his expression sombre.

She thought, If he takes the key out of my hand and comes into the flat with me now, I'm lost. She closed her eyes.

He took her hand from the door-jamb and placed it against his chest, under the tailored jacket. She could feel his heart hammering like a runner's. Her eyes flew open.

His eyes glittered. There was a faint flush along his cheekbones. Paula felt burned by the intensity of desire in his face.

Desire, she thought. Not love.

With a small cry of absolute despair, she tore her hand away from him and whisked inside the door.

CHAPTER EIGHT

PAULA didn't sleep well. In fact, she thought the next morning, she probably hadn't slept at all. She alternately curled under the duvet, and flung herself crossways across the wide bed. But neither was comfortable. Neither gave her respite from her galloping thoughts.

They weren't comfortable thoughts.

In the end she got up and trailed into the shadowed sitting-room, hugging her old towelling robe about her. She huddled into the corner of the sofa, tucking her feet under the cushions which had once brought her back to sanity by sliding to the floor.

Paula winced, remembering. They had so very nearly made love on that sofa. If love was the right word, she reminded herself drily. They had barely met, certainly didn't know each other. He had still been despising her at the time. And she? Well, she had been very angry, angrier than she had ever been in her life.

And yet . . . And yet . . . out of nowhere had come that electric awareness. As if they were two halves of a whole and needed nothing so much as to come together. As if she could think of nothing else until they had.

What sort of woman am I? Paula sank her head into her hands, her fingers pushing through the blonde tangle that was the result of her disturbed night. That, too, was unheard-of. Normally she went to bed with her hair neatly plaited.

Well, at least he wouldn't want me if he could see me now, Paula thought, trying to laugh at herself. But something told her that even that wasn't true. At the moment he wanted her any way he could get her. As she wanted him.

Paula began to cry, dreadful dry tears of bitterness. If only she were like Trish, she thought. If only she were still hopeful, still believed people could be loyal and honest; or, if they couldn't manage that, at least be kind.

But Neil had cured her of that. She had seen what sexual desire did to a man. How it made him tell lies he would have scorned in any other area of his life. How it blinded him to other people's feelings, including those of his desired object. How it drove him.

And Eduardo Mascherini was certainly driven. Paula knew compulsion when she saw it. Especially when she shared it.

'This,' she said grimly, 'could get nasty. I've left one job because of an emotional disaster. It's not going to happen again.'

She dreaded seeing him again. The morning of the next meeting with Isola's merchant bank, she was uncharacteristically sick. Looking at her wan face in the mirror, she thought that anyone who wanted to gossip about her relationship with Eduardo Mascherini would have some real evidence this time.

But nobody mentioned her pallor. Across the room she saw him regarding her frowningly while one of the bankers was talking. But he made no personal approach.

'This all looks very satisfactory,' one of the bankers told her patronisingly. 'If it works, of course.'

'It will work in law,' Paula told him coolly. 'The ongoing relationships, of course, are what matter. And that's up to Isola.'

'Of course.' He looked round. 'Well, gentlemen, I think that winds it up. I'll make the announcement this afternoon.'

Paula suppressed a sigh of relief. That meant that her part was done, at least for the time being.

As the meeting broke up, Eduardo touched her on the elbow.

'What have you been doing to yourself?'

She jumped and half turned to find him alarmingly close. Her heart began to pound as usual.

'What?'

'You look like death,' he told her frankly.

'Work.' Her reply was brief and discouraging.

Eduardo was not noticeably discouraged. 'You've lost weight,' he said with a frown.

It was true. Nobody else had noticed. Paula shrugged. He looked suddenly angry.

'Are you going to drive yourself into the ground just to spite me?'

'Don't be ridiculous.'

'I don't often suffer from remorse but you're fast teaching me,' he said wryly.

'Educational,' she said and made to push past him.

He stopped her with one arm across the doorway. He looked down at her searchingly.

'What is it, Paula?' he asked quietly. 'What did I do to scare you so?'

She looked after the other members of the group. But the meeting was dissolving cheerfully in the corridor without noticing that two of the principals had been left behind.

She looked at his determined expression and decided that nothing but the truth would do.

'I'm too old to play games,' she said in a low voice. 'The wrong temperament as well. But mostly too old.'

The heavy brows drew together. His whole expression demanded that she explain.

Paula sighed. She swung round, her back against the wall, and tipped her head up to look at him.

'I'm thirty-one, Eduardo,' she said quietly. 'I was happy enough. I'd settled down to getting my satisfaction out of my professional successes. Celibacy and a good career. It's not a bad life.'

Typically he picked up the one thing that made her vulnerable in that little speech. '*Was* happy enough?'

'You've stirred me up. I admit it.' Her eyes evaded his. 'You've made me—oh, discontented with my lot.'

His eyes were suddenly brilliant. 'Then——'

'I said you'd made me discontented,' Paula said swiftly. 'Not that you'd offered me anything that I wanted in place of it.'

'And what do you want?' he asked in a soft voice.

Paula bit her lip. She was not going to cry over him.

'Not to be your mistress.'

He moved sharply. She went on in a rapid voice before he could start arguing that black was white, 'Your game and your rules. I don't like them and I won't play by them. I'm a long-term lady, Eduardo. I work. I plan. I do that in relationships as well. If I get involved again I want the full works. Cats and dogs and kids and a husband to come home to. To have coming home to me.'

Her voice became suspended.

Eduardo looked stunned. He said in an undervoice, 'Paula...'

'Don't tell me I'm crazy. I know it's not going to happen.' She swallowed hard. 'I can take that. What I can't take is the cheap substitute.'

It was no good. She was going to cry. She dashed the back of her hand across her face furiously.

'Forgive me,' she said. 'I must go. I'm expecting a call.'

He stood back without protest. She caught a glimpse of the dark, inscrutable face as she shot out of the room. He looked shocked.

Presumably no one had ever asked him for marriage before, Paula thought, splashing cold water on her face. She tried to laugh. Her little outburst had certainly shaken him. There hadn't been a gleam of amusement in the grey eyes when she fled.

She inspected herself critically. Her eyes were faintly pink and puffy but she looked good enough as long as the office wasn't too alert. She could always say she had the beginnings of a cold, of course.

Back in her office, Sarah came in, looking severe. Sarah was probably her closest friend at work. Paula braced herself for an adverse comment on her appearance. But Sarah had other preoccupations.

'That dizzy Dora,' she began explosively.

In spite of herself, Paula grinned. Tragedies came and went but office politics continued unabated.

The subject of Sarah's complaint was the new team member, a pretty socialite whose profile was almost as stunning as her inherited pearls. She had a moderate degree and an elastic interpretation of her working hours. Sarah was convinced that she was Kit Marriott's way of handicapping the department that had produced the majority of the last quarter's profits. Marriott liked profit but, in her view, he thought it more important that his position in the firm stayed unassailable.

Paula soothed her and promised to speak to Antonia.

'You do too much,' Sarah grumbled. 'You ought to take that holiday. That would show them.'

After receiving Paula's note she had booked and cancelled Paula's trip to the health farm twice already.

Paula rubbed her eyes. 'When I've finished the Gardiner pleadings.'

Sarah sniffed. 'I'll believe it when I see it,' she said. But she didn't criticise further. Instead she took off the pile of notes for typing and papers for filing without demur.

Paula sat back in her chair sighing. At least Sarah, eagle-eyed though she was, hadn't detected the unwilling magnetism between her boss and the prestige client.

'That health farm looks more and more inviting,' she admitted to Sarah, later that day after three attempts to calculate her hours worked had ended in three different answers.

Her secretary sighed. 'Do you want me to ring them again? They've virtually got you on stand-by.'

But Paula shook her head. 'Maybe in a few days.'

But in a few days she had Kit Marriott in her office, playing with her embossed inkwell, gift of a grateful client, and making other plans.

'I need you to go to Italy,' he said bluntly.

It was in direct contravention of all professional courtesy to a partner and they both knew it. Paula raised her brows. Kit flushed.

'Look, I wouldn't ask if it wasn't important. We can't afford to lose the Isola account,' he said with the hint of pugnacity he could never quite hide, even when he was trying to be conciliatory.

Her heart started to thunder again.

'Isola?' she said softly.

Kit knew that tone of voice. He knew it was dangerous. He gave an artificial laugh.

'Now, Paula, don't go temperamental on me. It doesn't do the feminist cause any good at all. Just because you don't like the chap doesn't mean you can't do good work for him. He's very pleased with the Fortification project.' He eyed her speculatively. 'You never did tell me what you'd got against him, did you?'

'No, I didn't, did I?' Paula agreed coolly.

Kit frowned quickly. 'Not that it matters. Good God, you won't see Mascherini himself. This one is small beer for Isola.'

'Then you don't need a full partner to go to Italy, do you?' Paula said sweetly. 'Especially as it would seriously disrupt my own schedule. Send Adam.'

'I can't send an assistant.' Kit sounded genuinely scandalised. 'You may have to make decisions on the spot.' He took in her glacial expression and descended to wheedling. 'Look, forty-eight hours at the outside. You fly to Pisa. They'll meet you with the latest position. You read it in the car. Meeting with Isola, the Italian lawyers and the accountants. Back the next day.' He paused. Then, 'Look, you'll be dealing with the finance people. I don't think Eduardo's even there. He's been fixed in London all spring.'

That, as she had good reason to know, was true enough. Paula debated. It would not be good politics to give in easily, however.

She said acidly, 'And who covers here? Dolly Daydream? I do have one or two clients who are important to me, you know, even if you don't think they rank with Isola.'

'Are you telling me Antonia isn't up to the job?' Kit said swiftly.

Paula stared. She had been telling Kit that the new articled clerk was neither capable nor interested for months. But he was a member of the same club as her father.

'She goes tomorrow,' he said with a great display of decisiveness. 'She can go and do some matrimonial law.'

Paula's eyes narrowed. This was a major concession. But she kept her head. If Kit offered something, there was always more he was prepared to give if pushed.

'And who do I get in her place? Simon Rayne?'

Kit was plainly torn. Rayne was his personally selected articled clerk from this year's crop of graduates. Already he was turning in work worthy of a man with five years' experience.

'Only if he wants to come to you, of course.'

Paula was astonished. He must want her to go to Italy very badly indeed. 'And if he does?' she pressed.

Kit caved in. 'He's yours.'

'I'll go.' She buzzed Sarah. 'I'm going to Italy for Mr Marriott, Sarah. Will you liaise with his secretary and get the tickets and currency sorted out, please?' She added as an afterthought, 'I'll stay wherever the other advisers are staying.'

She had other orders for Sarah—like lunching Simon Rayne and making sure he saw the advantages of coming to their department, and finding out what was going on with Isola—but she didn't say any of that until Kit was gone.

It all happened a great deal faster than Paula was quite prepared for.

Sarah came in with the tickets later that afternoon. She was buzzing with suppressed excitement.

'It's all super-secret. That's why you're going, not Kit. You know what the Italian papers are like. They won't connect you with a new deal by Isola. But if Kit flew in they'd pick it up at once. It was Isola's idea. Kit,' she added with satisfaction, 'is spitting mad, so Jackie says.'

Imperceptibly Paula relaxed. It made sense; more sense anyway than her own instinctive reaction that this was Eduardo Mascherini's way of getting her on to his own territory and vulnerable.

'And Simon's been agitating to come to you for some time,' Sarah reported. 'So that's all right.' She handed over the folder of travel vouchers. 'You'll be met by one of the Isola chauffeurs. They'll take you to the hotel. The Isola people are being ultra-discreet about it. I've got a car to pick you up at eight tomorrow.'

Paula made a face. 'More packing. I can't even remember what I've got that's clean.'

Sarah was blithe. 'Get something new. The firm jolly well ought to pay. I'll clear it with Kit's secretary.'

Which was why Paula found herself driven out of the office at three-thirty with the business card of a small boutique in a Chelsea backstreet provided by Kit's ultra-sophisticated secretary.

'Get yourself kitted out,' Kit said briskly, putting his nose round the door to assure her the firm would pay. 'Then you can come back and sign the really urgent letters. After that, you go off and enjoy yourself.'

Paula looked at him with something approaching loathing. But she had got an admirable articled clerk out of the deal. She shrugged and went.

The women in the shop were surprisingly attentive. Paula normally bought clothes fast from one of the more impersonal exclusive shops. The degree of personal attention slightly unnerved her. So did their ideas about what constituted an acceptable professional wardrobe for a two-day stay in Italy.

Looking anxiously at her watch, she weighed the amount of time she had to argue and eventually decided to cut her losses. The clothes were all beautiful and she could well afford them. She would just have to tell Kit that she'd decided it was wrong for the firm to pick up the bill.

'Look,' she said at last, 'I'm in a hurry. I'll take the suit, the silk trousers and the cocktail frock. Pack them up and I'll have someone collect them. Just give me the bill.' And she proffered a credit card.

There was consternation. Paula sighed, looking at her watch again, while the saleswomen conferred among themselves.

Eventually the most senior said, 'I'm afraid we only accept credit cards from existing customers, Miss Castle.'

Paula's brows flew up at this contravention of every financial practice she had ever heard.

'Forgive me. Since we do not know you and we do know—er—Mr Marriott, will you forgive us if on this occasion...?' She trailed off into well bred but nevertheless firm murmurs of regret.

Paula shook her head and gave up.

'We will be happy to open an account for you, Miss Castle,' the saleswoman assured her consolingly.

'Fine,' said Paula absently. 'Though on my usual timetable I won't be buying clothes for another twelve months.'

The saleswomen all laughed politely. They obviously didn't believe her. It was clear that they found it inconceivable that a woman would buy new clothes annually—and that only if she found the time to go shopping, Paula thought. She shrugged.

'We look forward to seeing you again, madam,' she was assured, as she was ushered ceremoniously to the door and the unobtrusively ordered taxi. 'Perhaps we may have the honour...? Since we understand there is to be a wedding?'

'Your information network is to be congratulated,' Paula said, startled.

As far as she knew no one at Marriotts had made the connection between the forthcoming marriage of Mascherini's cousin and her own sister.

These keen-eyed *vendeuses*, however, were ahead in the game. Presumably it was part of their job, she thought vaguely.

'If I have time I shall certainly come back to choose something for the wedding.'

And that, she could see, truly shocked them. She got into the taxi, shaking her head at the strangeness of the way other people lived their lives.

She signed the letters that were waiting for her. There was only one case really outstanding and that she left Sarah strict instructions to call her about.

Sarah took the folders with their signed letters away from her.

'You can do with a break,' her secretary informed her kindly. 'Use it. This place doesn't fall apart if you're not here. Go home and have an early night.'

'I've got to pack. That'll take till midnight,' said Paula, grinning.

But when she got home she found that Isabel had not only collected the new clothes from the boutique, she had packed everything in a new suitcase with its complementary overnight case which she assured Paula was a present from the firm.

'The world's gone crazy,' said Paula. 'Since when do Marriotts care what my suitcase looks like?'

Isabel looked silently at the ancient battered brown affair with its myriad labels before transferring her eloquent gaze to the matching cream leather luggage. Paula gave a reluctant laugh.

'It's a conspiracy,' she complained. 'Everybody seems to want to turn me into a luxury article. You. Kit. The women in the boutique. Even Sarah. I suppose I shall understand it in time.'

It was prophetic. Though fortunately Paula didn't appreciate that at the time.

It was a good flight. They arrived slightly ahead of time. The small crowded airport seethed with people but the chauffeur was easy enough to identify in his sober uniform. He was also, slightly to Paula's embarrassment, carrying a placard with her name on it in Gothic black lettering.

She identified herself to him and was greeted ceremoniously. At a snap of his fingers, porters relieved her of her luggage. At another wordless command a girl detached herself from the throng and advanced on Paula with an enormous bouquet.

Paula, receiving armfuls of trailing jasmine and syringa, began to have a nasty suspicion.

'Thank you,' she said glacially.

The girl looked puzzled. Presumably the lady recipients of Eduardo Mascherini's mischievous floral tributes were usually more overwhelmed, thought Paula, her temper rising.

She let the temper rip. It felt healing. And anyway it was better than the flat panic which was the lurking alternative.

She allowed herself to be escorted to the stretched limousine and handed in with the ceremony that the chauffeur thought his professional standing decreed. Paula hardly noticed. She was busy rehearsing exactly what she would say to the author of all this unwanted opulence as soon as she saw him. She had no doubt that she was going to see him all too soon.

She carried on turning choice phrases over in her mind throughout the drive. It was long and taken at a hairraising pace that, if Paula had been less preoccupied, would have drawn a protest from her. As it was she barely noticed.

At last they turned off the *autostrada*, then off the main road on to a route that looked as if it was more used to carrying farm carts than the aristocratic Mercedes. They were climbing steadily. The track wound among trees, skirting precipices into a steep river valley.

The sun-soaked air was very still. Apart from the expensive purr of the engine there wasn't a sound. Paula stirred. If the Isola people wanted a discreetly out-of-the-way venue for their business meeting they certainly seemed to have found it.

'Where are we?'

The chauffeur smiled into the driving mirror and said something that sounded like a Roman baths. Paula repeated the question and got the same answer. She gave up.

At last the car bumped to a halt. She looked out of the window in bewilderment. She could see nothing but trees as far as the horizon. They appeared to be in some sort of wood.

She got out cautiously. At once her London heels sank into a concoction of twigs, dead leaves and almost dry soil. They were in a small, deserted clearing. In the distance, very faintly, she could hear the sound of water. There was no sign of a building of any sort.

'Hotel?' she asked the chauffeur without much hope. She wasn't really surprised when he shook his head. She sighed impatiently, looking round. To her left, the hill rose sharply, though the tree cover was too dense for her to see what lay beyond the wood. To her right, there was the steep slope to the valley with its musical stream.

'Beautiful,' said Paula drily. 'Just the place for international commercial negotiations.'

The chauffeur beamed, not understanding. He took her cases out of the boot and made for some steps that she had not made out among the trees.

Paula looked round again carefully. Not only were there no other cars in the clearing, there were no signs that there ever had been any other cars. Of course the rest of the party of advisers could be in whatever building

proved to be beyond those steps. Somehow, though, she
was losing faith in the other advisers.

Still, there was no point in refusing to move from the
Mercedes. She shrugged and followed the now invisible
chauffeur.

The house, when it came into view, was beautiful. It
had deep windows, almost to the ground, and great
wooden shutters, now closed against the inroads of the
afternoon sun.

The entrance hall was cool and dark and exquisitely
furnished with oak settles that she was almost certain
were antiques. Great copper urns of trailing fernery stood
about in alcoves. A crimson velvet-cushioned ecclesi-
astical seat was set to the left of an arch.

There was no sign of the chauffeur; or her cases. Nor
was there anything that might be a reception desk.

Looking about her, Paula made an unwelcome, though
not entirely unexpected discovery. It didn't feel like a
hotel. It felt like someone's home. Suspicion became
certainty.

She heard steps and saw a smiling woman approaching her.

'I would like,' Paula said grimly, 'to see Eduardo
Mascherini. Now.'

'Of course, *signorina*.' There was no sign of surprise.
'The Conte is in the garden. I will show you...'

'I'll find my way,' said Paula. This was not a conversation for which she wanted an audience.

But even that didn't cause surprise. Instead the woman
smiled—almost indulgently, Paula saw to her rising
fury—and indicated large double doors at the end of the
passageway, masked by half-closed shutters.

'Thank you,' said Paula between lips like ice.

The garden was blindingly bright. She stood in the
doorway, blinking. The trees, she saw, had been cleared,

to give a garden that was terrace after terrace. Box hedges
gave way to geraniums, which gave way to lilies and
foxgloves, which led to an orchard...

And there, on the third terrace down, amid orange
trees and bougainvillaea, was a cunningly contrived rock
pool. Only the brightness of the water revealed that it
was not a natural feature of the landscape. It was long
and curved like a scimitar into a willow-shaded grotto.
There was a lone swimmer, powering up and down like
an Olympic champion.

Paula set her teeth and began to descend the flights
of shallow steps.

He must have heard her coming. Before she had
reached the pool terrace, he pulled himself out of the
water. When she got to the top of the last steps, he was
shaking the droplets from his hair. In the afternoon sun,
his chest and shoulders gleamed like polished wood.

Paula was scarcely aware of it.

'What the hell,' she began furiously, 'do you think
you're playing at?'

Eduardo Mascherini tilted his head so that he could
look up at her. His eyes were dancing.

'Bad flight?' he said sympathetically. 'Get into your
swimsuit and join me.'

Paula ground her teeth audibly. 'I came here for a
business meeting. I didn't bring a swimsuit.'

'I think you'll find you did,' he said quietly.

She swept on. 'And I strongly resent being brought
here under what were clearly false pretences right from
the start.' Paula stopped as if she'd been shot. 'What
did you say?'

He repeated it obligingly. 'Unless Christine Marchand
has slipped up. Which is unlikely after all these years.'

Paula's mouth felt anaesthetised. Shock, she realised.

'How do you know where I bought my clothes?' she demanded in a dusty voice. But she knew the answer.

He ran lightly up the steps. He gave a slight, theatrical shudder. 'I don't. I know where I bought your clothes,' he corrected gently. He was amused. He touched her arm lightly. 'You couldn't stay here looking like prosecuting counsel the whole time, darling. You must see that. It puts me off.'

Paula looked blindly down into the glimmering water. She thought wistfully of pushing him into it. Unfortunately they were too far from it.

She withdrew her arm from the slight pressure of his hand.

'You mean you've tricked me out just as if I were one of your mistresses?' She didn't know if she was more hurt or angry. Let it be anger, she thought. Please, God, let it be anger. 'How *dare* you?'

He crossed his arms over an impressively muscular chest. His lips twitched.

'Not very original,' he murmured.

'I don't feel very original,' Paula flashed. 'I feel used and cheated and very, very angry.'

The heavy brows rose. 'I can see that. But why? You need a holiday, everyone agrees. It is my pleasure to provide the retreat for you in which to relax.'

'If I'd thought this was anything but business, I'd have—I'd have . . .'

'Yes?' He sounded idle enough but his eyes were watchful.

'I'd have seen you boiled in oil before I'd have come,' she hissed.

He threw back his head and laughed. He had a long muscular neck and a full-throated laugh. The joyous sound bounced off the surrounding hillsides, making her jump.

'I'm sure you would. But now you're here, what are you going to do about it?'

Paula glared. 'Go right back.'

He shook his head. 'I don't think so.'

She stiffened. 'Are you telling me I'm a prisoner?' she said incredulously.

The smile widened. The grey eyes touched her mouth with an expression as explicit as a kiss.

'Not my prisoner. Maybe your own.'

'You're crazy,' she said with conviction.

'I don't think so.' Eduardo was unmoved. He seated himself on the edge of a basin of small blue trailing flowers and swung one naked foot. 'After all, you must have realised as soon as the car stopped—if not before—that this wasn't going to be a lawyers' convention on the affairs of Isola. Why didn't you make Marco turn round and drive you back to the airport at once?' His eyes were steady. 'Or why didn't you go into the house and call your office; make them pick you up as soon as they could get a car out here?'

Paula bit her lip. Neither of those courses of action had ever occurred to her.

'But you didn't, did you?' asked that quiet, hateful voice.

She lifted her chin. 'I didn't believe even you could pull such a stunt.'

He laughed. 'Is that why you came looking for me the moment you got here?'

'I didn't. I——' But under the level gaze she stopped.

He touched her cheek.

'Oh, yes, you did.' It was almost tender.

'I was confused,' Paula said, trying to stay calm. 'Worried.'

'You were mad as a hornet,' he corrected her. 'And you came looking for me to pick a fight the moment

Marco let you out of the car. I should think you've been choosing your words ever since you realised the car wasn't taking you into Florence.'

Paula stared at him. It was chilling to realise not only that he was right but that he knew her so well.

She said with an effort, 'You got me here under false pretences. I'm not sure it wouldn't count as kidnapping in the courts. Of course I'm angry.'

'Ah, if it were only anger. It would be so much easier to deal with. Wouldn't it?' His voice was husky.

Something inside her flared into life. Paula began to feel alarmed.

'I don't know what you're talking about.'

He surveyed her. 'Would you say you were a reasonable person?'

'Of course.'

Although her throat felt tight and her heart was beating hard and painfully against her ribs, she was still a reasonable woman in full command of the situation. Or so Paula told herself.

'And does a reasonable person go looking for someone just to pick a fight the moment they arrive in a strange place?'

'I——'

He stood up. She had forgotten how tall he was. In the bright sunshine he towered over her, his shadow engulfing her like a magician's cloak. She put a hand to her throat to ease her breathing. His eyes looked very black and intent.

'Do you pick a lot of fights, Paula Castle?'

'Of course not.'

'But that's why you came looking for me.' His eyes locked with hers; held them. 'Wasn't it?'

'Not—not exactly,' she managed. She was breathing as if she had been running. Yet he hadn't so much as touched her.

'So you *didn't* come looking for me to pick a fight with me? Are you sure? No?' The black velvet voice sank. 'So why do you suppose you came looking for me the moment you got out of that car?'

Paula could only stare at him, mesmerised.

'For the same reason that I was coming to your room as soon as I realised the car was here?' he asked softly.

And reached for her.

CHAPTER NINE

PAULA was too startled to retreat. With an odd sort of fatalism she felt as if she had been coming to this moment, this place, for weeks without realising it. Ever since he had first talked his way into her flat, in fact, she thought. She closed her eyes as he bent dizzyingly close.

He said something against her skin which she couldn't make out. And then he was kissing her with a slow, connoisseur's pleasure that sent little tremors of warning up and down her spine. It was a warning that all her saner self was crying out to her to listen to.

But Paula was warm and dazzled and the arms holding her were very strong. For a moment it felt to her empty heart as if he loved her. As if she need never be alone again. With a soft sigh of acquiescence she gave herself up to the pleasure of it.

He sensed it at once. His arms tightened so that she was off balance, leaning against him. His mouth discovered the secrets of the pulse at her throat. Paula had never felt sensation like it. She was pliant and trusting as his hands moved. She had never felt so aware of her body. Sensation tingled from her thudding heart to her fingertips. He let one hand play lightly up her bare arm and she shuddered in startled delight, her lips parting.

'There,' Eduardo said caressingly.

Paula opened heavy eyes. The sun on his naked shoulders made him look as if he was made of bronze. His skin smelled of sun and the herbs of the garden. He was smiling down at her with an expression she'd never seen on his face before; half the same delight that she recognised in herself; half something surprised and watchful. As if he'd won a victory, she thought, and wasn't quite sure whether he could hold on to his prize.

She put up a gentle hand to touch his face in reassurance. And stopped. A *prize*? She felt a small chill.

He saw her hesitation. He took her hand and carried it to his lips.

'Don't.'

Paula's bewildered eyes searched his face. He was feathering the back of her hand with tiny kisses, watching her under his lashes. He looked amazingly handsome. And untrustworthy. The chill got stronger.

'Don't look like that,' he said softly. 'This was bound to happen.' He smiled.

The chill turned to ice. Paula pulled her hand away.

'You were bound to jump on me?' she said. She sounded a lot more breathless than she liked; and rather young and uncertain for a professional woman who knew her own mind.

From the look on his face he heard the same wavering in her voice that she did. He seemed hardly to have noticed her rejecting gesture. He looked amused, if anything. He certainly didn't look like a man who expected her to stick to resistance. If only she felt more certain of her ability to resist that skilled seduction herself, Paula thought, alarmed.

Don't be ridiculous, she reproached herself silently. You haven't been uncertain for years. You're an intelligent woman in charge of her own life. Don't let this man get to you.

She averted her eyes from those bare, tanned shoulders and said firmly, 'Being jumped on is not part of the deal. I don't expect to be treated like this.'

That disquieting amusement grew. 'Then you're very unrealistic,' Eduardo said calmly. 'Even if you can't see it for yourself, I've been telling you I'd get you into bed ever since we met.'

The ice solidified into an iceberg he was going to wreck himself on. Paula was so angry she wasn't even embarrassed.

'You will not,' she said between her teeth, 'get me into bed.' He chuckled. Her resolve grew rock-hard. 'You won't.' And at his patent disbelief she said mockingly, 'You want to watch that vanity, Eduardo.'

He shrugged those devastating shoulders. 'You're here in my house. For an unspecified period of time. As I've just proved, we can't keep our hands off each other. Where's the vanity?'

Paula clasped her hands tightly over her endangered shoulder-bag and glared at him.

'I have no trouble at all in keeping my hands off you,' she assured him sweetly. 'I'd regard it as unethical to do anything else.'

His eyebrows rose. 'Unethical?'

Paula set her jaw. 'I'm trying to remind you that I'm here as your legal adviser,' she said with restraint.

'Oh. That's OK, then,' he said, satisfied.

'And I don't indulge in affairs with clients,' she pursued, ignoring him.

He was watching her quizzically.

'I'm glad to hear it,' he said in patent approval.

Paula lost the battle to stay calm. 'Why are you doing this?' she almost wailed.

For a moment the handsome face sobered. He made as if to touch her. But then his hand fell to his side.

'You're tired and you've only just arrived,' he said. 'Maria Grazia will show you to your room and then we'll talk.'

She looked at him in despair. 'How do I get through to you? What do I have to say? No room. No talk. I'm leaving.'

His eyes flickered but he said nothing.

'There's no job for me here, is there?' she went on. 'You just told Kit Marriott to parcel me up and send me out here and by God he did. Have you no conscience at all?' She was nearly crying.

Eduardo flinched. 'It wasn't like that.'

Paula took hold of herself. 'The first time we met, you accused me and Trish of manipulating Franco. Do you remember that? Well, how do you think it compares? What have you done to me?'

She had every right to sound outraged, she thought, hearing herself. But it was more than outrage. It was a bleak sense of betrayal.

His face changed. 'Darling, that's nonsense.'

Betrayal? How could she feel betrayed by this man? He'd never given her any promises. Not even any implicit undertaking of fair dealing. He had raged at her the first time they met and he had teased and taunted her ever since. She neither liked nor trusted him. He was behaving exactly as his reputation and her own experience had led her to expect. So where was the betrayal? Why was she so hurt that he had plotted with Kit?

'Don't call me darling,' Paula said, glad suddenly that she could feel anger as well as the massive hurt.

In spite of her wretchedness her brain was working rapidly. *Why* did she feel betrayed by a man she had never trusted in the first place? It didn't make sense.

Plotting with Kit. Yes, that was it. She couldn't bear the thought that Eduardo had gone behind her back and plotted with her partner. They were equals in their battle, evenly matched opponents. It was cheating to enlist someone else who had nothing to do with their private affairs.

'But you are my darling,' he said softly.

Private affairs!

Paula looked at him with shocked eyes. Her anger evaporated in the unwelcome surge of realisation. She regarded this man as her private affair. Virtually as her own property.

Looking into cool grey eyes, she made a horrifying discovery. She was in love with him.

'Oh, dear God,' said Paula, the fight going out of her.

He saw the change in her at once. And, of course, took advantage of it, she thought bitterly.

'We are due for a long talk. But not yet. Come along. We'll find your room. You can put your head under the shower and calm down. Maybe then we'll both make more sense.'

Paula went with him silently. Quick though he was, he had not detected her revelation, she realised. She hoped she could manage to keep him in ignorance.

She didn't want to be in love with a laughing stranger who strolled around half-naked in the sunshine and made love to her with his eyes, even when he wasn't touching her. She didn't want to be in love with a man who was used to control and made people play his games by his rules. She didn't want to be in love with a man who saw love as a temporary diversion.

She didn't want to be in love again at all. Not with anyone. But especially not with Eduardo Mascherini.

He was too attractive. And he knew it. He was too powerful. He knew that too and used it shamefully. Why else was she here? Above all he was too experienced. His every move in her direction had proved that. And he had no conscience whatsoever about making those moves. What was it he had said? That he couldn't tolerate his cousin having a relationship with a woman he wanted himself?

Paula's heart was heavy. Neil had wanted her. He'd not had much of a conscience either. She'd ended up badly hurt, with her self-respect in ruins and her job untenable. All because she'd loved him. And it looked as if now she was facing something horribly similar.

She thought, startled, I'm thinking as if I'm already his mistress.

Only this time it would be worse. She'd have difficulty finding another partnership as good as this one, especially if it became common knowledge that she'd had an affair with an important client. Eduardo might feel honour bound to keep silence, of course, once it was over. She bit her lip.

He seemed to think an affair between them was inevitable. Had she started to accept it too?

They were mounting the shallow steps to the house. Eduardo looked down at her. He said shrewdly, 'I don't like this silence. Whenever you start to brood, I lose ground. What are you thinking?'

'I was wondering how discreet you were likely to be,' Paula said with truth. It was perhaps a little unwary of her.

His eyes flared suddenly, then narrowed. He stopped dead, searching her face. His expression was almost grim.

'Don't say things like that if you don't mean them,' he said at last, evenly. 'Do you?'

Paula was startled, as much by her own involuntary remark as by his reaction to it. Had he won so easily, then?

Her eyes fell under the onslaught of his.

'I thought not,' he said in an odd voice. 'Paula——'

But they were interrupted. The smiling woman who had met her earlier came on to the terrace. As soon as she saw Eduardo she burst into a torrent of agitated speech.

He frowned, then shrugged and replied swiftly. The woman nodded.

Turning to Paula, he said, 'I'm afraid our tête-à-tête will have to be postponed. Maria Grazia will show you to your room. I have to go out. I'll see you at dinner. *Ciao*.'

He was gone on silent feet almost before Paula had time to assimilate it. She looked after him, feeling oddly bereft.

Maria Grazia clicked her tongue. 'It is a disgrace the way they keep him running around, that family,' she said. 'But he will be back for dinner. He promised. The *signore* always keeps his promises.'

Paula's eyebrows climbed. She had taken the older woman for a family retainer and probably a simple peasant. Neither the sentiments nor the impeccable English bore this out.

'Er—you've known him long?' she asked, following.

The older woman took her into the cool interior and up a narrow staircase obviously parallel with the sweeping specimen Paula had already seen.

'Since his grandfather brought him back.'

'Brought him back?' Paula echoed. 'From where? Reform school?' she asked, thinking of his manifest lack of conscience.

Maria Grazia was not offended.

'He said you fought a lot,' she said in tones of congratulation.

'He fights,' Paula corrected ruefully. 'I defend myself.'

Maria Grazia took her along a corridor where the polished wooden floor creaked with every step.

'He can be tough,' she agreed. 'But he is fair, always.' Her pleasant face darkened. 'And more than fair to that family.'

Paula was intrigued. 'You don't care for them?'

'They don't care for him,' said Maria Grazia with emphasis. 'You know his father had two families?'

'He—er—he said something about it.'

'Signor Eduardo was from the first marriage. So he was legitimate. The family didn't know until his father died. And then all hell broke out.' Maria Grazia opened a door at the end of the corridor. 'Your room.'

'What sort of hell?' asked Paula, too interested to notice the splendours of the apartment before her.

The other woman shrugged. 'A war of succession, Eduardo calls it. The family was rich, you understand. There was the title. But, much more than that, there were businesses all over the world. His grandfather made him the sole heir with the proviso that he was to look after the other members of the family appropriately.' She snorted.

'Appropriately. What does that mean? They thought he was a simple peasant boy and would do what they told him.'

She looked at Paula under her lashes.

'Marry who they wanted,' she added carelessly. 'Always they were throwing people at him. Sometimes he thought the woman cared for him—and then found out that she was the protégée of one of his aunts and they had been plotting together. It is no wonder he marries nobody.'

Paula realised she was being given important information. She also realised that, though it hurt, it was kindly meant. Not, of course, that it mattered to her a jot if Eduardo Mascherini was not a marrying man. She had never thought he was. But it was surprisingly painful to have it spelled out for her by a kindly servant.

Maria Grazia sent her a shrewd look and said, 'Up to now, of course.'

Paula sketched a smile. 'Of course.'

She wandered over to the long windows and looked out. They gave a startling vista over the valley and the hillside beyond. In the distance she could hear the little river again. The sun was dropping towards the west, casting deep shadows into the gorge. Everywhere there were trees, just bursting into leaf.

'It is the *signore's* favourite view,' Maria Grazia informed her.

Paula accepted the information with a non-committal tilt of the head. 'What are the trees?' she asked.

'Mainly chestnut. We burn the logs here. Though in this season it is mainly in the drawing-room at night. That is why the house smells like this,' Maria Grazia explained. She picked up Paula's overnight case which was standing behind the door and swung it on to a webbed stool which she had flicked open expertly. 'You can have a fire in here now, though, if you would like. The *signore* does not normally care for it, so we don't light fires for guests, but if you would prefer...'

'No, that's fine,' Paula said hurriedly. 'I'm sure I'll be warm enough.'

Maria Grazia's eyebrows rose abruptly and were as abruptly schooled to a more sober expression.

'Of course, *signorina*,' she murmured. 'You would like to rest now, I'm sure. Dinner is at nine. The *signore* will be back by then.'

She opened Paula's smart new suitcase with a deft click. Then she left, closing the door with care behind her.

Paula looked without favour at the contents of her case. Had she bought a garment suitable for dining in an elegant country house while making it plain to the master of that house that she was not his for the taking?

She gave a short mirthless laugh. Such a dress didn't exist in the history of the universe. It would have to be basic black and her feminine instinct for survival. Eduardo Mascherini was going to take a lot of convincing. Come to that, thought Paula sighing, so was she. Those few short moments in his arms had revived all sorts of feelings that she would be much more comfortable without.

'Full body armour, that's what you need,' she told her reflection dourly, noticing the disarray caused by her journey for the first time.

Or most of it caused by the journey. Absently, Paula straightened the fair fronds that were beginning to drift round her neck; and then stopped. He would have seen that; he had probably caused them to come loose from their restraining pins in the first place. Her pale skin flushed deeply. She glared at the reflected face as if it were an enemy.

'You are not a child,' she told herself out loud. 'And Eduardo Mascherini is not invincible. He may be amusing himself. He probably is. Well, hold on to that. When he touches you, just remember that he is an unprincipled seducer to whom you are the newest challenge. Stay just that. A challenge. There's no need to give him the victory on a plate. Or at all, if we're lucky. Keep your head and we'll come out of this all right.'

She devoutly hoped she was right.

Her first stroke of luck was that the warm bath she took to wash away the grime of the journey sent her into a drowsy state of well-being. She trailed out of the austere pine-walled bathroom and collapsed on the huge bed, still wrapped in her bath-towel. At some point, still debating what to wear, she drifted into sleep.

Her second stroke of luck was that Eduardo didn't come back. Or at least not until she was dressed and, primed with the driest of Martinis, waiting for him in front of the chestnut log fire.

She was not entirely sure about the basic black. It was only when she had got it on that she remembered the boutique's idea of basic included a sculpted line that made her waist look impossibly small and a burst of sequinned spirals on the severe lapel that drew attention to a neckline that plunged more than she remembered too. She'd hesitated in front of the mirror. But in the end she'd decided to go with it.

The decision was a little defiant. But the dress made her look good, she thought, more feminine than she had felt for a long time. She wasn't going to deprive herself of that just because Eduardo Mascherini might interpret the dress as an invitation. It was a perfectly respectable dress, she argued. And if he got the wrong idea, she'd brain him.

But in fact when he joined her he didn't pass any comment on her appearance at all.

He came in so quietly that Paula didn't hear him. She was sitting on a small embroidered stool in front of the fire, staring into the flames. Maria Grazia had offered to switch on the lamps but Paula had waved her away. She wanted to savour the soft shades of the twilit view from the tall terrace windows. When she became aware of Eduardo standing in the shadows at the other end of the room, she gave a slight start and swung round, suddenly tense again.

He strolled forward. 'No, don't get up. You looked too peaceful. Did I startle you?'

But Paula was on her feet already. She felt obscurely that it was somehow important to keep her eyes on a level with his.

He was looking very handsome. Paula thought, with a slight drying of her throat, that she had never seen him look so handsome. She had seen him in riding breeches, in tracksuit and in the formal suiting of the City, as well as this afternoon's baroque display of tanned skin and muscle. But in the dark trousers and deep-collared, open-necked shirt he was devastating. She felt her skin tingle with unwelcome awareness.

One eyebrow rose. Paula realised she was staring. She looked away, confused.

'What are you sitting in the dark?'

She shrugged. 'Oh, I liked the view. The light. I wanted to watch the sun go down.'

'Was it a good one?'

'The sunset?' She gave a rueful laugh. 'It looked pretty good to me. I don't have much to compare with it. You don't get a lot of sunsets in London. And I'm usually asleep on aeroplanes when we fly into them.'

He said curiously, 'Do you enjoy it? The continent hopping, I mean.'

She shrugged again. 'It comes with the job.'

'And the job?'

'It pays the bills.'

He made an abrupt, dismissive movement. 'Don't be flip with me, Paula,' he said, surprising her. 'Your job, your career—do you enjoy that? Is it important to you?'

There was something in his tone that demanded an answer; and a considered one.

Paula said slowly, 'My job has always been important. First because it was all that kept Trish and me eating. Then because I did it well. I like finding solutions to things. It's pleasing. And then—well, then something happened in my life and I needed a bit of an ego boost. That's when my job got inextricably tied up with my self-respect, I suppose.'

'You mean that's when you got obsessive,' Eduardo interpreted.

Paula gave a startled laugh. 'You sound like my sister.'

'That's not surprising. I've been briefed by your sister.'

'Oh.' Paula bit her lip. For some reason she found this piece of news disquieting.

'Yes, "oh",' he mimicked. He sounded almost angry for a moment. 'It isn't what I like. But you didn't leave me much choice. You wouldn't tell me anything, would you?'

He took a step closer. She was forced to tilt her head to look up into his face. It felt like defiance. In spite of the hostility she thought she could detect in his tone, in the wavering firelight his expression was unreadable.

'Have you told me anything about yourself?' she countered.

'You had only to ask.'

Eduardo looked down at her silently for a long moment. Paula had the impression of steady eyes. And an implacable will. She drew a shaky breath.

'Were you ever going to tell me?' he asked.

She jumped. 'Tell you what?'

'About Neil Roberts,' he said quietly.

Paula turned to stone. For a moment she felt as if she literally could not breathe: as if all the air was building up in her lungs and would explode before she could let it out of her paralysed throat.

How could he have found out? Nobody knew at work. Nobody. Kit couldn't have told him that, whatever else he might have been willing to do for his favourite client. So how had Eduardo Mascherini extracted her most painful secret?

'Magic?' she demanded out of a harsh anger. 'Or do you use private detectives?'

His hand came out to her involuntarily, then fell to his side.

'Trish told me.'

Paula swallowed painfully. Of course. Trish found it easy to confide, to tell her hurts to strangers. Only in the past she had not added Paula's hurts to those she was prepared to discuss.

'Thank you, Trish,' Paula muttered.

'I had to drag it out of her,' he said as if he was consoling her.

Paula found she was shivering. Shock, she thought. And the realisation that as an opponent this man had no scruples at all.

Her head came up in pride. Her voice when she spoke was like a whip. 'Of course, I realise that, as your future relation by marriage, I can't expect to have my privacy respected any more——' even in the firelight she saw him wince '—but what I don't understand is why you bothered.'

He said wryly, 'You're the only woman in the world of whom I'd believe that.'

It was Paula's turn to wince. She was probably the first woman he'd met who didn't know how his sophisticated games were played. Even if she'd wanted to play. The trouble was, ever since that long, sweet kiss on the terrace, her resolution had been wavering.

He must have seen her hesitation. He said in a reasonable tone, 'Why don't we sit down and discuss this quietly over a drink?'

'I've got a drink,' said Paula in a cold fury that was more than half at her own weakness.

'Well, I haven't.' He sounded wry. 'And I think I'm going to need one.' He went over to the tray Maria Grazia had brought in earlier. Ice chinked. With his back to her he said, 'Oh, for God's sake, stop seething and give me the facts.'

'Facts?'

He turned back. 'Neil Roberts,' he reminded her. 'That's who it is, isn't it?'

'I don't know what you mean.'

Eduardo gave her a measuring look. 'Yes, you do. I didn't realise at first. But it's as if you carry an invisible chaperon with you. Every time I touch you, there he is.'

Paula whitened.

'What I want to know,' Eduardo said gently, 'is why.'

She said with an effort, 'You're imagining it.'

'No.' His voice was meditative. 'No. When I first met you I thought you were the classic career woman, not interested in anything but your own ambition. But you're not. I don't even think you're very ambitious. And you're not heartless. So—you're thirty-one, beautiful as an angel, and the moon isn't lonelier. I wanted to know why. And Trish said—ask you about Neil Roberts.' He looked at her gravely. 'I'm asking.'

Paula swallowed. She didn't answer. She couldn't. The palms of her hands were clammy.

Eduardo's eyes narrowed. 'All right. We'll look at it another way. You're not really happy about where you're going, are you, Paula?'

She had heard that tone from opponents negotiating before court hearings; the best opponents.

She cleared her throat. To her relief her voice seemed to be working again. She said warily, 'What do you mean, where I'm going?'

He leaned casually against a heavy oak table, swirling the liquid in his glass. She heard the ice chink again. But he didn't drink. He seemed to be thinking.

'Well, you're not really going anywhere, are you? Or not anywhere new. Just more of the same.'

'*What*?'

'You're young to be a partner in a London firm, of course,' he mused. 'Even a small firm. Very young. You must have worked bloody hard to get there. I admire that, of course. But——' He stopped and looked down at his glass, his mouth slanting wryly. 'And that's exactly how you'll go on. I've been there myself. Working till you can't see straight. Night and day. Across the Atlantic so many times you don't know where you are till you see which side the cabs drive.'

It was Paula's turn to wince. His eyes lifted suddenly. She felt pinned like a butterfly on green baize.

'That first time I saw you, you were so tired you were a danger to yourself and everyone else around you.'

She was on the defensive at once. 'I wasn't. Maybe I was a bit tired. But——'

'You let me muscle into your apartment without so much as a token protest,' he said flatly. 'I could have been a burglar. A rapist. Anything. You just weren't awake enough to see the risk.'

There was not, of course, any answer to that. It was something Paula had been conscious of at the time. And even more so in retrospect. She had never behaved like that in her life before. She had even wondered whether it was because, as he kept insisting, there really was some invisible bond between them which, in her jet-lagged state, she had instinctively recognised. But she wasn't going to tell Eduardo Mascherini that, naturally. Instead she went on the attack. 'A burglar would have been a lot less trouble,' she flung at him.

His mouth was grim. 'And a rapist?'

She shrugged. 'I can look after myself. I don't just go to the gym to ride stationary bicycles, you know.'

There was an unflattering silence while he surveyed her.

'Karate? You're out of your mind. I wasn't armed and I wasn't violent. And you didn't even remember your karate when I kissed you. What do you think would have happened if you'd been really frightened?'

Paula stared at him, shocked. It was true. She hadn't even thought of her self-defence techniques. She had been too carried away on unaccustomed sensation.

'You didn't want me to kiss you,' he reminded her, misinterpreting her silence. 'But you didn't know how to stop me.'

She looked away from him suddenly.

'OK. I'll give you that,' she said in a muffled voice. 'What's the point of this?'

He said softly, and he cannot have known how cruelly, 'But you told me yourself what you wanted, Paula. Cats and dogs and kids. A husband to come home to.'

She flinched as if she'd unwarily put her hand in the fire behind them. Eduardo saw it. Before he could move she said in a tight voice, 'That was nonsense and you know it. I'm a career woman through and through.'

He gave her a disbelieving look. 'Are you telling me that's how you want to run your life?'

Paula contemplated pointing out that she wasn't telling him anything—and discarded the idea at once. Eduardo Mascherini was impervious to snubs.

She said instead with deliberate sarcasm, 'Are you offering me an alternative?'

He went very still. In the shadows she thought she saw his mouth quirk. She was already beginning to shake her head, wishing she hadn't tried to be clever, as he said coolly, 'I might.'

The trap was such an easy one to see. Hardly a trap at all, really. And she had walked right into it. She fought to retrieve her position.

'Oh, no,' said Paula, at her most mocking. 'No, I don't believe it. Exchange a career for being millionaire Mascherini's playmate? Now why didn't I think of that?'

He said calmly, 'You have a commonplace mind.'

'It wasn't *my* idea.'

'And you leap to conclusions,' he went on, unheeding. 'I've noticed that right from the start. Isn't that very dangerous for a lawyer?'

'I do not leap to conclusions,' Paula said between her teeth. 'You've been flourishing your sex appeal at me since the first moment we met. Don't try to deny it.'

Eduardo looked amused. 'Is that what I've been doing? And I thought I was being honest and open as we're all supposed to be in our relationships these days. I don't think you're very liberated, my darling.'

She caught her breath in a hiss. The unexpected meaningless endearment hurt like a blow on a bruise.

'Don't call me that,' Paula told him quietly. 'I'm as liberated as I want.'

He strolled over to her and put one hand under her chin, forcing her to meet his eyes.

'You don't know what you want,' he said softly.

The dark eyes were dizzyingly close. It was a matter of pride to stare straight back without letting her eyes fall. Or, more important, fill with the weak tears she could already feel gathering.

'If you mean I don't want to be the latest crushed opponent in your sexual tournament, you're absolutely right,' she flung back at him.

He looked startled. '*Opponent*? Good God, do you think everything's a battle, woman?'

Her eyes darted fire. It was better than crying. He shook his head, looking down at her.

'You do,' he said on a note of discovery. 'You know, we've got to do something about this. You've got a one-track mind and one-track emotions. It's not healthy.' He sounded angry; but not desperate. Not as if he cared too much.

Paula broke the eye contact.

'Thank you very much for your support,' she said awfully.

'Any time.' His tone was soft. She could have hit him. 'Now when are you going to let me love you?'

It was the last straw. Paula could feel the volcanic eruption building as precisely as if she were watching a wave crash to shore. It was rather exhilarating.

She told him what she thought of his manners, morals and manoeuvres. She told him she had never liked rich men and he had confirmed all her prejudices. She said he was without sense or understanding.

He laughed.

'I wouldn't let you love me if you were the last man on earth,' she finished, in a low, cold voice that was more telling than any shouting would have been.

Eduardo was unmoved. 'You don't mean that. It's just a convenient cliché. We'll discuss it over dinner.'

'I do not want any dinner,' Paula told him in a voice that brooked no argument. 'I'm going to bed.'

He looked pained. She went to the door.

'And another thing. I'm leaving tomorrow morning. I'll sit in that damned airport until there's a flight to London. If you won't call me a cab, I'll walk. And I'm never coming anywhere near you again. Do I make myself clear?'

He met her angry eyes. To her outraged disbelief, Paula saw that his were dancing.

'I've never been so insulted in my life,' he prompted.

There was nothing dignified to say. And the only thing she could think of to do involved laying hands on him. Which, Paula knew, would not be wise.

She flung the double doors open with a flourish worthy of an invading army and marched out. They swung shut behind her with a bang that rang through the house. It gave her a measure of satisfaction. It was small consolation, however, for the indisputable fact that Eduardo Mascherini had won again.

CHAPTER TEN

THE night was dark. Sitting in the window looking out into the black valley, Paula thought she had never seen such darkness. The stars showed intermittently behind the scudding clouds. But the only light was that cast on to the terrace from the room in which Eduardo was taking his solitary dinner.

She stared at that light until her eyes ached. It was a constant temptation to go downstairs again; to tell him whatever he wanted to know; to let matters take whatever course they would. To surrender, she reminded herself grimly.

That was what Eduardo wanted: her unconditional surrender. He said it wasn't a battle but experience had taught her otherwise. No matter what he said, she had seen that triumphant look in his face when he'd thought she was going to succumb. Even if she hadn't, she had felt it in his kiss. Total domination, that was what he wanted.

'Never again,' said Paula out loud.

She might be in love with him but she still had to survive. And being Eduardo's discarded entertainment would be unimaginably worse than after Neil Roberts left her.

In fact, she realised, with a little start, she had almost forgotten Neil. Eduardo had pushed him out of her mind and her heart. If it weren't for the valuable lessons she had learned at his hands about the injuries all too easily inflicted on a woman in love, Neil would be an irrelevance.

She turned away from the window with a sigh. If only Eduardo loved her. If only he didn't speak of wanting and nothing else. Or if only she were braver.

Other women had affairs and survived after all. She was neither an untried girl nor a fool. Why wouldn't it work for her?

Paula sighed deeply. She didn't know the answer. She only knew the fact: that she had let Eduardo invade her heart. Given his track record and what he obviously expected in the way of a casual relationship, it would be crazy to let it go any further.

The trouble is, I'm not casual, Paula thought. If I were... But I'm not. Oh, lord, I wish I were at home.

She closed the shutters against the light spilling out on to the terrace and went to bed.

She lay in the lavender-scented sheets, listening to the noises of the alien countryside and the even more alien house. She thought she heard Eduardo's step on the stair and turned over restlessly. If only... If only...

She must have slept because she came suddenly and shockingly awake at a strange sound. It was horribly close. She strained to listen.

It came again: a soft rustling sound. Paula struggled up on to one elbow and stared into the deep shadows. The bed creaked. The rustling stopped.

Her eyes widened disbelievingly. A pool of darkness coalesced into a human shape; came towards her. Paula fell back among the pillows.

'What are you doing here?'

'Where else should I be?' Eduardo said softly. 'This is my room.'

Paula's heart lurched. 'What?'

She thought frantically. When she had left him she had run like mad. Had she mistaken the room? How could she? The pine bathroom was the same, surely. And the view.

Her suitcase? Had her suitcase been there? But she hadn't thought to check. She had sat in darkness, dreaming about him. And then she had flung off her clothes and fallen into bed.

She hauled the sheet up to her breasts, startled.

He said quietly, 'You're right, of course. This is the only way.'

Paula went perfectly still. She held her breath. For a moment she had a blazing image of herself and Eduardo entwined in the embrace of acknowledged lovers. Her whole body clenched in unbearable excitement.

She said harshly, as much to herself as to him, 'No.'

The bed creaked as he sat on the side of it. He didn't attempt to touch her.

'Lost your nerve?' He didn't sound angry. He sounded interested. And something else. Paula shivered.

'I didn't mean ... I didn't realise ...'

'It's a big step for you, isn't it?' Eduardo sounded almost dispassionate.

'I——'

In the shadows his body was a darker shadow, electric and vital. Paula felt her mouth go dry. She swallowed convulsively. Even though he wasn't touching her, she could feel the heat of him along her skin.

'Don't be afraid, darling. You've got this far.'

'I haven't,' she said. 'I mean, I didn't know. Oh, lord.' Her breathing was fast and shallow. She pressed a hand over her fluttering heart. 'Look, it was dark. I don't know this house. I thought—I didn't know this was your room.'

Eduardo ignored her stammering excuses. He seemed almost not to have heard.

'I'm in as deep as you, you know.'

If only that were true, thought Paula. She must have made some small movement. He leaned forward, scanning her pale face in the darkness.

'It's true. And I'm not giving up now. Or ever.' It sounded like a vow.

She was shaken. 'What?'

'However long it takes. The rest of our lives if necessary.'

Paula didn't pretend to misunderstand him. It sounded like a sentence to torture, she thought: to have what you really wanted held out to you permanently—only, at an impossible price.

She whispered, 'Please don't talk like that.'

'Why not? We were made for each other. You know that as well as I do.' In the darkness she could sense his sudden frustration. 'You're a fighter. You're brave. I saw that from the first. It's one of the things I——' He broke off. 'What is it that frightens you so about this?'

Loving you unloved, she could have said. She didn't. She swallowed. 'Look, Eduardo, you don't really know me...'

'Oh, yes, I do,' he said softly.

'You think you do. But...'

'I do. Don't forget I've seen you fighting like a tigress for your sister's happiness. I know you're brave and clever and funny. And when you love, you love forever.'

Paula found she had nothing to say. She stared at the pale blur in the darkness that was his face and felt the earth crumble under her.

He put out a hand and caressed her cheek very gently. His voice was low.

'Love me.'

There was a shivering silence. Paula closed her eyes in anguish. This was dreadful. It was so tempting. But it would cost her her whole life.

'I can't *afford* it,' she said at last in a suffocated voice.

The hand on her cheek stilled.

'*Why*?' Eduardo asked, as if it was wrenched out of him.

She was beyond argument. Her whole body was shaking with the need to be close to him; more than close.

'Self-respect,' she managed through lips that trembled so much, the words were hardly distinguishable.

He swore. Paula winced.

'Neil—Neil left me with no sense of self-worth at all. It took eight years to rebuild. I can't—I *can't* put it on the line again,' she said almost pleadingly. 'Don't ask me to.'

This time the silence screamed.

Then he said in a deadly voice, 'If that's what you want.'

Paula felt the tension inside her release like a snapped spring. Which was why she was completely unprepared when his arms closed round her.

'What...?' she began into a warm shirtfront. His heart was thundering against her.

'I've stopped asking,' he said. 'If you want me to make the decision, then by God I will.'

He put a hand under her chin and forced her to look up at him. His mouth closed on hers.

Paula tried to fight. But she was off balance, exhausted by the internal struggles of the last hour and her deepest self didn't want to fight him anyway.

She knew it wasn't sensible. She knew she'd probably pay for this for the rest of her life. But it was heaven to give herself up to the strength of his arms and the slow seduction of his kiss.

They fell back among the tangled sheets. Eduardo slid the sheet away from her clutching hands with an unhurried movement that did nothing to disguise his determination. Paula didn't even try to resist. She even helped him.

He kissed the length of her arm, from wrist to collarbone, in a slow savouring of her that was somehow shocking and yet the height of her dreams. Her skin felt as if it transformed into gold wherever he touched. His mouth moved on her throat. Paula's head fell back.

He said something against her skin. It sounded as if he was laughing again. Of course he would, she thought. He had won. But in the haze of spun gold delight that his hands were weaving Paula was beyond caring.

He drew the back of his hand down her skin, from breast to the cool curve of hip and thigh. Paula jumped. At once his hand fell away and he was kissing her, his mouth taking slow possession of her mind. She sighed.

He repeated the languid caress. This time Paula shivered like a stroked cat. Suddenly she became aware of a tension building within her that was entirely new. Startled, her eyes flew open. Her fingers clenched involuntarily on his shoulders.

Eduardo raised his head.

'Darling,' he said huskily. 'Tell me you want this.'

Paula's arms rose of their own accord to cradle his head. She didn't even think of resistance.

'Oh, yes,' she said on a voiceless whisper.

He began to touch her again, with shattering care, until she was arching and weeping in his arms, crying out for him not to stop until... until...

Until the world exploded, as he cried out her name on a note almost of anguish, and she fell into the silence of eternity.

The silence was broken by birdsong. Turning over among a crazy disposition of sheets and pillows, Paula blinked awake. She felt strange. Her body felt oddly weightless while her head seemed to be ringing with too many lights and colours. She had a feeling of absolute sensuous delight. It was amazing.

She stretched. A pillow fell squashily to the floor. She blinked again, coming further awake. She looked round the room blankly. It was dark except for a line of light like a knife-edge along the wooden floor. Puzzled, she turned her head and saw that it was the sun coming in between two wooden shutters.

In a flash memory came back. And with it the common sense she had so recklessly abandoned last night. She sat bolt upright in shock.

The room, she saw, was empty except for herself and the all too obvious evidence of last night's loss of control. The sheets looked to be knotted inextricably and there was more than one pillow on the floor. With them appeared to be every single thing Eduardo had been wearing, including his shoes.

Of Eduardo himself, however, there was not a trace.

Cautiously Paula edged out of bed, huddling the maltreated sheet round her. She went to the door of the bathroom, which was ajar, and advanced her nose to the edge of the door. But her caution was unnecessary. The bathroom was empty too.

It was a relief, Paula assured herself. She scrambled into her clothes without care. It was just as well Eduardo had gone. If she had seen him this morning, before she had had the time to wake up properly and remember, she could well have betrayed herself. He wouldn't want declarations of love, not now that he had established the relationship that he wanted. On his terms. Complete victory.

She fled to her own room. It was only two doors down the passage. Not difficult to find. If only she had found it last night.

No doubt he would have further plans for her, Paula thought, stuffing last night's dress into her suitcase. She looked at it with loathing. What was it he had said? That the clothes had been bought by him, not Marriotts at all? She thought of the sophisticated wardrobe with which the boutique had provided her and winced. He had seen to it that they had dressed her like the toy she was, she thought savagely: a toy for Eduardo Mascherini to play with.

I have got to get out, she thought.

She looked round the room a little desperately. There was her shoulder-bag. It contained her passport and airline tickets and, she hoped, enough money to get her back to the airport if she could only find a village with a resident taxi. She would need more comfortable shoes than she had worn last night. But there were some low-heeled pumps in the bigger case.

She would have to leave the rest of her luggage. But, since Eduardo had paid for it, he could dispose of it as well.

She found the desired footwear, slung the bag over her shoulder and let herself quietly out of the bedroom. The polished hall floor creaked, in spite of all her care. But nobody appeared to question or stop her.

She went down the staircase and out on to the terrace, after a slight struggle with the lock of one of the windows. It was, she realised, very early. She found she could see the road from the terrace. She also saw that if she went down through the garden she could rejoin it at the level of the valley floor, cutting out all the bends and sweeps of the mountain road. She set off.

She had been walking for over an hour when she realised ruefully that the landscape had been deceptive. The garden was steep, steeper when she was no longer walking down the steps between the formal terraces. As the sun got higher, the dew disappeared and she began to feel distinctly hot. She took off the jacket of her suit and looped it over her shoulder.

In the end it took more than two hours to walk to the village. At least, she thought, that meant that people were awake. Children were going to school and the café was opened for her by a surprised-looking woman carrying vegetables.

Paula asked for a coffee in careful Italian. It was produced with prompt kindness but there was no disguising the curiosity. When she asked about a taxi, the curiosity leaped to boiling point. Fortunately her Italian wasn't good enough to understand the questions.

She had difficulty in understanding the answers too. But eventually she managed to decipher that the village's only taxi driver was collecting an old lady from hospital. He would be back later. Until then, she could only wait. Perhaps breakfast? Paula agreed weakly.

The extraordinary sense of physical well-being had not worn off, in spite of her walk, in spite of her wretchedness. Paula took her cappuccino out into the sunshine and watched the farm vehicles going off to market. It was a beautiful scene, she thought drowsily. And if Eduardo were here with her it would be quite perfect.

She jumped. What was she thinking of? Eduardo was not offering companionship in roadside cafés, or anywhere else for that matter. He was offering smart clothes and a brief snatch of heaven in his arms: for a while. So there was no point in sitting here dreaming about something that was pure wish-fulfilment.

But last night felt like love, something stubborn inside Paula said.

No, it didn't, said the even more stubborn, reasoning side of Paula. You just wanted it to feel like love.

There was a step behind her. She took no notice. The café proprietor had been washing the tables. Paula had twice refused more rolls, more coffee. But the steps stopped. There was a scraping as one of the iron chairs was pulled out.

Paula looked up, startled, squinting into the sun at a dark shirt and jeans on a tall frame. The taxi driver?

'If I'd known you wanted to go out for breakfast,' Eduardo said levelly, 'I would have joined you.'

In spite of all rational Paula's arguments, her heart leaped at the sight of him. Irrational Paula seemed to be in charge again. She couldn't prevent her smile of welcome. It was pure instinct. A husband to come home to, she thought. That hurt. Her smile died.

He didn't smile back anyway.

'I didn't expect to find you gone this morning,' he told her in a bleak voice.

Paula looked away. 'Didn't you? Why not? Is it only men who are allowed to run out?'

The look he gave her wasn't flattering. 'You're confusing me with Neil Roberts again.'

Paula bit her lip, failing to meet his eyes.

'Is that what this is about?' he persisted. 'Running out on me before I can leave you? Competitive indifference?'

There was enough truth in that to make her wince.

He said quietly, 'My dear, I told you it wasn't a battle. It's not a competition either.'

Her eyes lifted at that. 'Are you telling me that you didn't want me—on your own terms, of course—and the hell with what I wanted?' she demanded scornfully.

The grey eyes were the colour of steel.

'Are you telling me you didn't want me? After last night?' he countered.

Paula flushed. The memories were too close; and uncomfortably explicit, with him sitting opposite her.

'I do not deny,' she said carefully, 'that I lost my head a little last night.'

'No,' he said quite gently.

'What?' Disconcerted, she stared at him.

'No, you didn't lose your head. You found it.'

She gave a mirthless laugh. 'By going to bed with you?'

'By making love with me,' he corrected.

'You must think I'm an awful fool,' she said bitterly. 'Do you really think that's the summit of experience any woman can aspire to?'

For a moment he closed his eyes as if he was in pain. Then he banged his fist down so hard that the iron table rocked.

'You are being wilfully destructive. God knows why I love you,' he said in a harsh tone. For once his accent was showing, Paula noticed, hardly taking in what he said. 'I know this man hurt you. But——'

'Love me?' she echoed a split-second later.

But Eduardo had lost his enviable temper at last.

'Has the rest of the world got to go on taking his punishment?' he demanded furiously.

'Love *me*?'

'It's yourself you hurt most.'

'You *can't* love me,' she said, bewildered. 'Nobody could. I work too much and I'm boring and I shout at people. You just want a brief affair.'

'If you give me a chance,' said Eduardo Mascherini, his voice suddenly lilting with laughter, 'I'll make you feel more loved than Cinderella.'

Paula scanned the handsome face and saw he meant it. The landscape seemed to shimmer suddenly.

'You said I had a one-track mind,' she reminded him, wanting him to convince her. 'And one-track emotions.'

'Because I wasn't getting anywhere with you. You wouldn't listen to me. Wouldn't talk to me. Don't you recognise frustration when you see it?'

'I don't believe it.'

'My darling,' he said, taking her hand firmly, 'you have been driving me quietly out of my mind since the first time I kissed you. This determination of yours not to see what was going on was way out of my experience. When Trish told me how you'd been hurt, I began to understand a little. But even then—you wouldn't let me near you.'

His hand brushed her cheek.

'I know why you didn't want to get involved again. When you care, you care too much. I know. I understand. And if it were anyone but me I'd say you were right.'

She blinked rapidly.

'But not me, my darling,' he said gently. 'I need you, Paula. I've never said that to anyone else. I never expected it to happen. But when you stood there and shouted me down because I was attacking your sister——' he brushed his thumb across her quivering lip '—I saw real feeling. I thought then, I need her in my life. She's mine.'

Paula remembered the electricity between them, even in that first furious encounter. She looked down.

'I suppose I knew,' she admitted at last in a low voice.

The grey eyes darkened. 'I thought you did. That's why that one-track rejection of yours had me half mad. You just kept saying no, there's nothing, no, I don't want you, when I knew...'

She shook her head. 'But I didn't want it to be true. I couldn't handle it. I knew that.'

Eduardo was very still.

'Was that how you felt last night?' There was real pain in the quiet voice.

Her hand went out to him. He didn't see it.

'No,' said Paula. 'Oh, no. But the consequences. I know a lot about the consequences of unrequited love. They'd break me.' She bit her lip. 'I'm sorry.'

'Unrequited . . . ?'

'You've never said you loved me.' Paula smiled sadly. 'I didn't expect it. That was your game, your rules. But, you see, I need more than a temporary affair.'

'You told me,' he said. His eyes were brilliant suddenly. 'A long-term lady. You startled me then, I admit. You made me think about what it was I was doing. And I found out I was pretty long-term too. About you.'

Paula stared at him, hardly believing her ears.

'I won't pretend that I wanted that from the beginning,' he said steadily. 'You have to understand, my darling. A lot of women have wanted to marry me. Not because of my charm. The only way I felt sure that a woman wanted me for myself was if we kept our options open and she only came to me when it was mutual. No strings. No settlements. I'm not proud of it. But can you understand?'

'Yes,' said Paula.

She sensed a loneliness that made her own life look positively full of love. At least she and Trish had relied on each other, never doubted each other.

'Maybe you do,' he said at last. 'What you said, you made me think. I realised I wanted the same. Wanted to come home to you.' He closed his eyes. 'And last night I thought I'd proved it.'

This time she took his hand between her own. His eyes flew open. Paula lifted his hand to her face and stroked her cheek against it. 'She's mine,' she repeated softly.

It sounded wonderful.

Eduardo searched her face. 'Permanently,' he said carefully. He hesitated. 'It was a shock to find you'd managed to shrug it off and leave.'

'It wasn't quite like that.' Paula bit her lip. She let go his hand. Looking down, she began to trace the wrought-iron pattern of the table. 'You see, Neil—well, he never stayed the night with me. We were lovers, or I thought we were, but——' She swallowed.

'And you woke up alone this morning and thought I was the same?'

She looked up quickly. The handsome face was twisted.

'Not consciously,' she said in quick remorse. 'Not deliberately. It's just that it was—sort of what I expected, I suppose. By then I knew that I hadn't loved Neil. I couldn't handle what I felt for you but I knew the rejection was going to be worse. I just had to get away. I couldn't face seeing you, pretending that it was all right. I felt as if I'd lost a terribly important battle.'

'My darling,' said Eduardo, 'don't you know we're on the same side? If you lose, I lose.'

Paula searched his face. He was very grave.

'If you love me,' he said steadily, 'you'll marry me.'

'I——'

'I asked you last night to love me,' he reminded her softly. 'I meant it. Can't you?'

Paula made a discovery: being in love was easy once you trusted the man you were in love with. She drew a long breath and leaned forward, smiling into his eyes.

'I'll consider it,' she said against his mouth. 'If you promise to wake up with me tomorrow morning.'

Eduardo gave a great shout of uninhibited laughter, surging to his feet. He kicked the iron table aside as if it were matchwood and took Paula into a comprehensive embrace.

'Every morning,' he vowed.

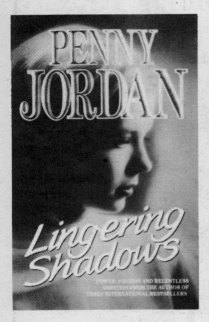

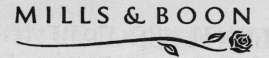

MILLS & BOON

Next Month's Romances

Each month you can choose from a wide variety of romance with Mills & Boon. Below are the new titles to look out for next month, why not ask either Mills & Boon Reader Service or your Newsagent to reserve you a copy of the titles you want to buy – just tick the titles you would like and either post to Reader Service or take it to any Newsagent and ask them to order your books.

Please save me the following titles: Please tick   ✓

Title	Author	
AN UNSUITABLE WIFE	Lindsay Armstrong	
A VENGEFUL PASSION	Lynne Graham	
FRENCH LEAVE	Penny Jordan	
PASSIONATE SCANDAL	Michelle Reid	
LOVE'S PRISONER	Elizabeth Oldfield	
NO PROMISE OF LOVE	Lilian Peake	
DARK MIRROR	Daphne Clair	
ONE MAN, ONE LOVE	Natalie Fox	
LOVE'S LABYRINTH	Jessica Hart	
STRAW ON THE WIND	Elizabeth Power	
THE WINTER KING	Amanda Carpenter	
ADAM'S ANGEL	Lee Wilkinson	
RAINBOW ROUND THE MOON	Stephanie Wyatt	
DEAR ENEMY	Alison York	
LORD OF THE GLEN	Frances Lloyd	
OLD SCHOOL TIES	Leigh Michaels	

If you would like to order these books in addition to your regular subscription from Mills & Boon Reader Service please send £1.90 per title to: Mills & Boon Reader Service, Freepost, P.O. Box 236, Croydon, Surrey, CR9 9EL, quote your Subscriber No:................................... (If applicable) and complete the name and address details below. Alternatively, these books are available from many local Newsagents including W H Smith, J Menzies, Martins and other paperback stockists from 8 April 1994.

Name:...

Address:...

....Post Code:.............................

To Retailer: If you would like to stock M&B books please contact your regular book/magazine wholesaler for details.

You may be mailed with offers from other reputable companies as a result of this application.
If you would rather not take advantage of these opportunities please tick box ☐